GREEN TEA

MR. JUSTICE HARBOTTLE

JOSEPH SHERIDAN LEFANU

TRUE SIGN
PUBLISHING HOUSE

Published by True Sign Publishing House
Address: SY. No. 21/2 & 21/3, Sonnenahalli,
Krishnarajapura, Bengaluru,
Karnataka - 560049 India
E-mail: truesignbooks@gmail.com
Website: www.truesign.in

Green Tea

Author: Joseph Sheridan Lefanu

ISBN: 978-81-19179-81-7

First Edition: 2023

CONTENTS

1. **GREEN TEA** **4**

   PROLOGUE **5**

   CHAPTER - I 7

   CHAPTER - II 11

   CHAPTER - III 14

   CHAPTER - IV 17

   CHAPTER - V 20

   CHAPTER - VI 23

   CHAPTER - VII 26

   CHAPTER - VIII 29

   CHAPTER - IX 32

   CHAPTER - X 35

   CONCLUSION **40**

2. **MR. JUSTICE HARBOTTLE** **42**

   PROLOGUE **43**

   CHAPTER - I 45

   CHAPTER - II 49

   CHAPTER - III 54

   CHAPTER - IV 58

   CHAPTER - V 62

   CHAPTER - VI 65

   CHAPTER - VII 68

   CHAPTER - VIII 72

   CHAPTER - IX 76

GREEN TEA

PROLOGUE

Martin Hesselius, the German Physician

Though carefully educated in medicine and surgery, I have never practised either. The study of each continues, nevertheless, to interest me profoundly. Neither idleness nor caprice caused my secession from the honourable calling which I had just entered. The cause was a very trifling scratch inflicted by a dissecting knife. This trifle cost me the loss of two fingers, amputated promptly, and the more painful loss of my health, for I have never been quite well since, and have seldom been twelve months together in the same place.

In my wanderings I became acquainted with Dr. Martin Hesselius, a wanderer like myself, like me a physician, and like me an enthusiast in his profession. Unlike me in this, that his wanderings were voluntary, and he a man, if not of fortune, as we estimate fortune in England, at least in what our forefathers used to term "easy circumstances." He was an old man when I first saw him; nearly five-and-thirty years my senior.

In Dr. Martin Hesselius, I found my master. His knowledge was immense, his grasp of a case was an intuition. He was the very man to inspire a young enthusiast, like me, with awe and delight. My admiration has stood the test of time and survived the separation of death. I am sure it was well-founded.

For nearly twenty years I acted as his medical secretary. His immense collection of papers he has left in my care, to be arranged, indexed and bound. His treatment of some of these cases is curious. He writes in two distinct characters. He describes what he saw and heard as an intelligent layman might, and when in this style of narrative he had seen the patient either through his own hall-door, to the light of day, or through the gates of darkness to the caverns of the dead, he returns upon the narrative, and in the terms of his art and with all the force and originality of genius, proceeds to the work of analysis, diagnosis and illustration.

Here and there a case strikes me as of a kind to amuse or horrify a lay reader with an interest quite different from the peculiar one which it may possess for an expert. With slight modifications, chiefly of language, and of course a change of names, I copy the following. The narrator is Dr. Martin Hesselius. I find it among the voluminous notes of cases which he made during a tour in England about sixty-four years ago.

It is related in series of letters to his friend Professor Van Loo of Leyden. The professor was not a physician, but a chemist, and a man who read history and metaphysics and medicine, and had, in his day, written a play.

The narrative is therefore, if somewhat less valuable as a medical record, necessarily written in a manner more likely to interest an unlearned reader.

These letters, from a memorandum attached, appear to have been returned on the death of the professor, in 1819, to Dr. Hesselius. They are written, some in English, some in French, but the greater part in German. I am a faithful, though I am conscious, by no means a graceful translator, and although here and there I omit some passages, and shorten others, and disguise names, I have interpolated nothing.

CHAPTER - I

Dr. Hesselius Relates How He Met the Rev. Mr. Jennings

The Rev. Mr. Jennings is tall and thin. He is middle-aged, and dresses with a natty, old-fashioned, high-church precision. He is naturally a little stately, but not at all stiff. His features, without being handsome, are well formed, and their expression extremely kind, but also shy.

I met him one evening at Lady Mary Heyduke's. The modesty and benevolence of his countenance are extremely prepossessing.

We were but a small party, and he joined agreeably enough in the conversation, He seems to enjoy listening very much more than contributing to the talk; but what he says is always to the purpose and well said. He is a great favourite of Lady Mary's, who it seems, consults him upon many things, and thinks him the most happy and blessed person on earth. Little knows she about him.

The Rev. Mr. Jennings is a bachelor, and has, they say sixty thousand pounds in the funds. He is a charitable man. He is most anxious to be actively employed in his sacred profession, and yet though always tolerably well elsewhere, when he goes down to his vicarage in Warwickshire, to engage in the actual duties of his sacred calling, his health soon fails him, and in a very strange way. So says Lady Mary.

There is no doubt that Mr. Jennings' health does break down in, generally, a sudden and mysterious way, sometimes in the very act of officiating in his old and pretty church at Kenlis. It may be his heart, it may be his brain. But so it has happened three or four times, or oftener, that after proceeding a certain way in the service, he has on a sudden stopped short, and after a silence, apparently quite unable to resume, he has fallen into solitary, inaudible prayer, his hands and his eyes uplifted, and then pale as death, and in the agitation of a strange shame and horror, descended trembling, and got into the vestry-room, leaving his congregation, without explanation, to themselves. This occurred when his curate was absent. When he goes down to Kenlis now, he always takes care to provide a clergyman to share his duty, and to supply his place on the instant should he become thus suddenly incapacitated.

When Mr. Jennings breaks down quite, and beats a retreat from the vicarage, and returns to London, where, in a dark street off Piccadilly, he inhabits a very narrow house, Lady Mary says that he is always perfectly well. I have my own opinion about that. There are degrees of course. We shall see.

Mr. Jennings is a perfectly gentlemanlike man. People, however, remark something odd. There is an impression a little ambiguous. One thing which certainly contributes to it, people I think don't remember; or, perhaps, distinctly remark. But I did, almost immediately. Mr. Jennings has a way of looking sidelong upon the carpet, as if his eye followed the movements of something there. This, of course, is not always. It occurs now and then. But often enough to give a certain oddity, as I have said, to his manner, and in this glance travelling along the floor there is something both shy and anxious.

A medical philosopher, as you are good enough to call me, elaborating theories by the aid of cases sought out by himself, and by him watched and scrutinised with more time at command, and consequently infinitely more minuteness than the ordinary practitioner can afford, falls insensibly into habits of observation, which accompany him everywhere, and are exercised, as some people would say, impertinently, upon every subject that presents itself with the least likelihood of rewarding inquiry.

There was a promise of this kind in the slight, timid, kindly, but reserved gentleman, whom I met for the first time at this agreeable little evening gathering. I observed, of course, more than I here set down; but I reserve all that borders on the technical for a strictly scientific paper.

I may remark, that when I here speak of medical science, I do so, as I hope some day to see it more generally understood, in a much more comprehensive sense than its generally material treatment would warrant. I believe the entire natural world is but the ultimate expression of that spiritual world from which, and in which alone, it has its life. I believe that the essential man is a spirit, that the spirit is an organised substance, but as different in point of material from what we ordinarily understand

     GREEN TEA

by matter, as light or electricity is; that the material body is, in the most literal sense, a vesture, and death consequently no interruption of the living man's existence, but simply his extrication from the natural body—a process which commences at the moment of what we term death, and the completion of which, at furthest a few days later, is the resurrection "in power."

The person who weighs the consequences of these positions will probably see their practical bearing upon medical science. This is, however, by no means the proper place for displaying the proofs and discussing the consequences of this too generally unrecognized state of facts.

In pursuance of my habit, I was covertly observing Mr. Jennings, with all my caution—I think he perceived it—and I saw plainly that he was as cautiously observing me. Lady Mary happening to address me by my name, as Dr. Hesselius, I saw that he glanced at me more sharply, and then became thoughtful for a few minutes.

After this, as I conversed with a gentleman at the other end of the room, I saw him look at me more steadily, and with an interest which I thought I understood. I then saw him take an opportunity of chatting with Lady Mary, and was, as one always is, perfectly aware of being the subject of a distant inquiry and answer.

This tall clergyman approached me by-and-by; and in a little time we had got into conversation. When two people, who like reading, and know books and places, having travelled, wish to discourse, it is very strange if they can't find topics. It was not accident that brought him near me, and led him into conversation. He knew German and had read my Essays on Metaphysical Medicine which suggest more than they actually say.

This courteous man, gentle, shy, plainly a man of thought and reading, who moving and talking among us, was not altogether of us, and whom I already suspected of leading a life whose transactions and alarms were carefully concealed, with an impenetrable reserve from, not only the world, but his best beloved friends—was cautiously weighing in his own mind the idea of taking a certain step with regard to me.

I penetrated his thoughts without his being aware of it, and was careful to say nothing which could betray to his sensitive vigilance my suspicions respecting his position, or my surmises about his plans respecting myself.

We chatted upon indifferent subjects for a time but at last he said:

"I was very much interested by some papers of yours, Dr. Hesselius, upon what you term Metaphysical Medicine—I read them in German, ten or twelve years ago—have they been translated?"

"No, I'm sure they have not—I should have heard. They would have asked my leave, I think."

"I asked the publishers here, a few months ago, to get the book for me in the original German; but they tell me it is out of print."

"So it is, and has been for some years; but it flatters me as an author to find that you have not forgotten my little book, although," I added, laughing, "ten or twelve years is a considerable time to have managed without it; but I suppose you have been turning the subject over again in your mind, or something has happened lately to revive your interest in it."

At this remark, accompanied by a glance of inquiry, a sudden embarrassment disturbed Mr. Jennings, analogous to that which makes a young lady blush and look foolish. He dropped his eyes, and folded his hands together uneasily, and looked oddly, and you would have said, guiltily, for a moment.

I helped him out of his awkwardness in the best way, by appearing not to observe it, and going straight on, I said: "Those revivals of interest in a subject happen to me often; one book suggests another, and often sends me back a wild-goose chase over an interval of twenty years. But if you still care to possess a copy, I shall be only too happy to provide you; I have still got two or three by me—and if you allow me to present one I shall be very much honoured."

"You are very good indeed," he said, quite at his ease again, in a moment: "I almost despaired—I don't know how to thank you."

"Pray don't say a word; the thing is really so little worth that I am only ashamed of having offered it, and if you thank me any more I shall throw it into the fire in a fit of modesty."

Mr. Jennings laughed. He inquired where I was staying in London, and after a little more conversation on a variety of subjects, he took his departure.

CHAPTER - II

The Doctor Questions Lady Mary and She Answers

"I like your vicar so much, Lady Mary," said I, as soon as he was gone. "He has read, travelled, and thought, and having also suffered, he ought to be an accomplished companion."

"So he is, and, better still, he is a really good man," said she. "His advice is invaluable about my schools, and all my little undertakings at Dawlbridge, and he's so painstaking, he takes so much trouble—you have no idea—wherever he thinks he can be of use: he's so good-natured and so sensible."

"It is pleasant to hear so good an account of his neighbourly virtues. I can only testify to his being an agreeable and gentle companion, and in addition to what you have told me, I think I can tell you two or three things about him," said I.

"Really!"

"Yes, to begin with, he's unmarried."

"Yes, that's right—go on."

"He has been writing, that is he was, but for two or three years perhaps, he has not gone on with his work, and the book was upon some rather abstract subject—perhaps theology."

"Well, he was writing a book, as you say; I'm not quite sure what it was about, but only that it was nothing that I cared for; very likely you are right, and he certainly did stop—yes."

"And although he only drank a little coffee here to-night, he likes tea, at least, did like it extravagantly."

"Yes, that's quite true."

"He drank green tea, a good deal, didn't he?" I pursued.

"Well, that's very odd! Green tea was a subject on which we used almost to quarrel."

"But he has quite given that up," said I.

"So he has."

"And, now, one more fact. His mother or his father, did you know them?"

"Yes, both; his father is only ten years dead, and their place is near Dawlbridge. We knew them very well," she answered.

"Well, either his mother or his father—I should rather think his father, saw a ghost," said I.

"Well, you really are a conjurer, Dr. Hesselius."

"Conjurer or no, haven't I said right?" I answered merrily.

"You certainly have, and it was his father: he was a silent, whimsical man, and he used to bore my father about his dreams, and at last he told him a story about a ghost he had seen and talked with, and a very odd story it was. I remember it particularly, because I was so afraid of him. This story was long before he died—when I was quite a child—and his ways were so silent and moping, and he used to drop in sometimes, in the dusk, when I was alone in the drawing-room, and I used to fancy there were ghosts about him."

I smiled and nodded.

"And now, having established my character as a conjurer, I think I must say good-night," said I.

"But how did you find it out?"

"By the planets, of course, as the gipsies do," I answered, and so, gaily we said good-night.

Next morning I sent the little book he had been inquiring after, and a note to Mr. Jennings, and on returning late that evening, I found that he had called at my lodgings, and left his card. He asked whether I was at home, and asked at what hour he would be most likely to find me.

Does he intend opening his case, and consulting me "professionally," as they say? I hope so. I have already conceived a theory about him. It is supported by Lady Mary's answers to my parting questions. I should like much to ascertain from his own lips. But what can I do consistently with good breeding to invite a confession? Nothing. I rather think he meditates one. At all events, my dear Van L., I shan't make myself difficult of access; I mean to return his visit tomorrow. It will be only civil in return for his politeness, to ask to see him. Perhaps something may come of it. Whether much, little, or nothing, my dear Van L., you shall hear.

CHAPTER - III

Dr. Hesselius Picks Up Something in Latin Books

Well, I have called at Blank Street.

On inquiring at the door, the servant told me that Mr. Jennings was engaged very particularly with a gentleman, a clergyman from Kenlis, his parish in the country. Intending to reserve my privilege, and to call again, I merely intimated that I should try another time, and had turned to go, when the servant begged my pardon, and asked me, looking at me a little more attentively than well-bred persons of his order usually do, whether I was Dr. Hesselius; and, on learning that I was, he said, "Perhaps then, sir, you would allow me to mention it to Mr. Jennings, for I am sure he wishes to see you."

The servant returned in a moment, with a message from Mr. Jennings, asking me to go into his study, which was in effect his back drawing-room, promising to be with me in a very few minutes.

This was really a study—almost a library. The room was lofty, with two tall slender windows, and rich dark curtains. It was much larger than I had expected, and stored with books on every side, from the floor to the ceiling. The upper carpet—for to my tread it felt that there were two or three—was a Turkey carpet. My steps fell noiselessly. The bookcases standing out, placed the windows, particularly narrow ones, in deep recesses. The effect of the room was, although extremely comfortable, and even luxurious, decidedly gloomy, and aided by the silence, almost oppressive. Perhaps, however, I ought to have allowed something for association. My mind had connected peculiar ideas with Mr. Jennings. I stepped into this perfectly silent room, of a very silent house, with a peculiar foreboding; and its darkness, and solemn clothing of books, for except where two narrow looking-glasses were set in the wall, they were everywhere, helped this somber feeling.

While awaiting Mr. Jennings' arrival, I amused myself by looking into some of the books with which his shelves were laden. Not among these, but immediately under them, with their backs upward, on the floor, I lighted upon a complete set of Swedenborg's "Arcana Caelestia," in the original Latin, a very fine folio set, bound in the natty livery which theology affects, pure vellum, namely, gold letters, and carmine edges. There were paper markers in several of these volumes, I raised and placed them, one after the other, upon the table, and opening where these papers were placed, I read in the solemn Latin phraseology, a series of sentences indicated by a pencilled line at the margin. Of these I copy here a few, translating them into English.

"When man's interior sight is opened, which is that of his spirit, then there appear the things of another life, which cannot possibly be made visible to the bodily sight."...

"By the internal sight it has been granted me to see the things that are in the other life, more clearly than I see those that are in the world. From these considerations, it is evident that external vision exists from interior vision, and this from a vision still more interior, and so on."...

"There are with every man at least two evil spirits."...

"With wicked genii there is also a fluent speech, but harsh and grating. There is also among them a speech which is not fluent, wherein the dissent of the thoughts is perceived as something secretly creeping along within it."

"The evil spirits associated with man are, indeed from the hells, but when with man they are not then in hell, but are taken out thence. The place where they then are, is in the midst between heaven and hell, and is called the world of spirits—when the evil spirits who are with man, are in that world, they are not in any infernal torment, but in every thought and affection of man, and so, in all that the man himself enjoys. But when they are remitted into their hell, they return to their former state."...

"If evil spirits could perceive that they were associated with man, and yet that they were spirits separate from him, and if they could flow in into the things of his body, they would attempt by a thousand means to destroy him; for they hate man with a deadly hatred."...

"Knowing, therefore, that I was a man in the body, they were continually striving to destroy me, not as to the body only, but especially as to the soul; for to destroy any man or spirit is the very delight of the life of all who are in hell; but I have been continually protected by the Lord. Hence it appears how dangerous it is for man to be in a living consort with spirits, unless he be in the good of faith."...

"Nothing is more carefully guarded from the knowledge of associate spirits than their being thus conjoint with a man, for if they knew it they would speak to him, with the intention to destroy him."...

"The delight of hell is to do evil to man, and to hasten his eternal ruin."

A long note, written with a very sharp and fine pencil, in Mr. Jennings' neat hand, at the foot of the page, caught my eye. Expecting his criticism upon the text, I read a word or two, and stopped, for it was something quite different, and began with these words, Deus misereatur mei—"May God compassionate me." Thus warned of its private nature, I averted my eyes, and shut the book, replacing all the volumes as I had found them, except one which interested me, and in which, as men studious and solitary in their habits will do, I grew so absorbed as to take no cognisance of the outer world, nor to remember where I was.

I was reading some pages which refer to "representatives" and "correspondents," in the technical language of Swedenborg, and had arrived at a passage, the substance of which is, that evil spirits, when seen by other eyes than those of their infernal associates, present themselves, by "correspondence," in the shape of the beast (fera) which represents their particular lust and life, in aspect direful and atrocious. This is a long passage, and particularises a number of those bestial forms.

CHAPTER - IV

Four Eyes Were Reading the Passage

I was running the head of my pencil-case along the line as I read it, and something caused me to raise my eyes.

Directly before me was one of the mirrors I have mentioned, in which I saw reflected the tall shape of my friend, Mr. Jennings, leaning over my shoulder, and reading the page at which I was busy, and with a face so dark and wild that I should hardly have known him.

I turned and rose. He stood erect also, and with an effort laughed a little, saying:

"I came in and asked you how you did, but without succeeding in awaking you from your book; so I could not restrain my curiosity, and very impertinently, I'm afraid, peeped over your shoulder. This is not your first time of looking into those pages. You have looked into Swedenborg, no doubt, long ago?"

"Oh dear, yes! I owe Swedenborg a great deal; you will discover traces of him in the little book on Metaphysical Medicine, which you were so good as to remember."

Although my friend affected a gaiety of manner, there was a slight flush in his face, and I could perceive that he was inwardly much perturbed.

"I'm scarcely yet qualified, I know so little of Swedenborg. I've only had them a fortnight," he answered, "and I think they are rather likely to make a solitary man nervous—that is, judging from the very little I have read—I don't say that they have made me so," he laughed; "and I'm so very much obliged for the book. I hope you got my note?"

I made all proper acknowledgments and modest disclaimers.

"I never read a book that I go with, so entirely, as that of yours," he continued. "I saw at once there is more in it than is quite unfolded. Do you know Dr. Harley?" he asked, rather abruptly.

In passing, the editor remarks that the physician here named was one of the most eminent who had ever practised in England.

I did, having had letters to him, and had experienced from him great courtesy and considerable assistance during my visit to England.

"I think that man one of the very greatest fools I ever met in my life," said Mr. Jennings.

This was the first time I had ever heard him say a sharp thing of anybody, and such a term applied to so high a name a little startled me.

"Really! and in what way?" I asked.

"In his profession," he answered.

I smiled.

"I mean this," he said: "he seems to me, one half, blind—I mean one half of all he looks at is dark—preternaturally bright and vivid all the rest; and the worst of it is, it seems wilful. I can't get him—I mean he won't—I've had some experience of him as a physician, but I look on him as, in that sense, no better than a paralytic mind, an intellect half dead. I'll tell you—I know I shall some time—all about it," he said, with a little agitation. "You stay some months longer in England. If I should be out of town during your stay for a little time, would you allow me to trouble you with a letter?"

"I should be only too happy," I assured him.

"Very good of you. I am so utterly dissatisfied with Harley."

"A little leaning to the materialistic school," I said.

"A mere materialist," he corrected me; "you can't think how that sort of thing worries one who knows better. You won't tell any one—any of my friends you know—that I am hippish; now, for instance, no one knows— not even Lady Mary—that I have seen Dr. Harley, or any other doctor. So pray don't mention it; and, if I should have any threatening of an attack, you'll kindly let me write, or, should I be in town, have a little talk with you."

I was full of conjecture, and unconsciously I found I had fixed my eyes gravely on him, for he lowered his for a moment, and he said:

 Green Tea

"I see you think I might as well tell you now, or else you are forming a conjecture; but you may as well give it up. If you were guessing all the rest of your life, you will never hit on it."

He shook his head smiling, and over that wintry sunshine a black cloud suddenly came down, and he drew his breath in, through his teeth as men do in pain.

"Sorry, of course, to learn that you apprehend occasion to consult any of us; but, command me when and how you like, and I need not assure you that your confidence is sacred."

He then talked of quite other things, and in a comparatively cheerful way and after a little time, I took my leave.

CHAPTER - V

Dr. Hesselius is Summoned to Richmond

We parted cheerfully, but he was not cheerful, nor was I. There are certain expressions of that powerful organ of spirit—the human face—which, although I have seen them often, and possess a doctor's nerve, yet disturb me profoundly. One look of Mr. Jennings haunted me. It had seized my imagination with so dismal a power that I changed my plans for the evening, and went to the opera, feeling that I wanted a change of ideas.

I heard nothing of or from him for two or three days, when a note in his hand reached me. It was cheerful, and full of hope. He said that he had been for some little time so much better—quite well, in fact—that he was going to make a little experiment, and run down for a month or so to his parish, to try whether a little work might not quite set him up. There was in it a fervent religious expression of gratitude for his restoration, as he now almost hoped he might call it.

A day or two later I saw Lady Mary, who repeated what his note had announced, and told me that he was actually in Warwickshire, having resumed his clerical duties at Kenlis; and she added, "I begin to think that he is really perfectly well, and that there never was anything the matter, more than nerves and fancy; we are all nervous, but I fancy there is nothing like a little hard work for that kind of weakness, and he has made up his mind to try it. I should not be surprised if he did not come back for a year."

Notwithstanding all this confidence, only two days later I had this note, dated from his house off Piccadilly:

Dear Sir,—I have returned disappointed. If I should feel at all able to see you, I shall write to ask you kindly to call. At present, I am too low, and, in fact, simply unable to say all I wish to say. Pray don't mention my name to my friends. I can see no one. By-and-by, please God, you shall hear from me. I mean to take a run into Shropshire, where some of my people are. God bless you! May we, on my return, meet more happily than I can now write.

About a week after this I saw Lady Mary at her own house, the last person, she said, left in town, and just on the wing for Brighton, for the London season was quite over. She told me that she had heard from Mr. Jenning's niece, Martha, in Shropshire. There was nothing to be gathered from her letter, more than that he was low and nervous. In those words, of which healthy people think so lightly, what a world of suffering is sometimes hidden!

Nearly five weeks had passed without any further news of Mr. Jennings. At the end of that time I received a note from him. He wrote:

"I have been in the country, and have had change of air, change of scene, change of faces, change of everything—and in everything—but myself. I have made up my mind, so far as the most irresolute creature on earth can do it, to tell my case fully to you. If your engagements will permit, pray come to me to-day, to-morrow, or the next day; but, pray defer as little as possible. You know not how much I need help. I have a quiet house at Richmond, where I now am. Perhaps you can manage to come to dinner, or to luncheon, or even to tea. You shall have no trouble in finding me out. The servant at Blank Street, who takes this note, will have a carriage at your door at any hour you please; and I am always to be found. You will say that I ought not to be alone. I have tried everything. Come and see."

I called up the servant, and decided on going out the same evening, which accordingly I did.

He would have been much better in a lodging-house, or hotel, I thought, as I drove up through a short double row of sombre elms to a very old-fashioned brick house, darkened by the foliage of these trees, which overtopped, and nearly surrounded it. It was a perverse choice, for nothing could be imagined more triste and silent. The house, I found, belonged to him. He had stayed for a day or two in town, and, finding it for some cause insupportable, had come out here, probably because being furnished and his own, he was relieved of the thought and delay of selection, by coming here.

The sun had already set, and the red reflected light of the western sky illuminated the scene with the peculiar effect with which we are all familiar.

The hall seemed very dark, but, getting to the back drawing-room, whose windows command the west, I was again in the same dusky light.

I sat down, looking out upon the richly-wooded landscape that glowed in the grand and melancholy light which was every moment fading. The corners of the room were already dark; all was growing dim, and the gloom was insensibly toning my mind, already prepared for what was sinister. I was waiting alone for his arrival, which soon took place. The door communicating with the front room opened, and the tall figure of Mr. Jennings, faintly seen in the ruddy twilight, came, with quiet stealthy steps, into the room.

We shook hands, and, taking a chair to the window, where there was still light enough to enable us to see each other's faces, he sat down beside me, and, placing his hand upon my arm, with scarcely a word of preface began his narrative.

CHAPTER - VI

How Mr. Jennings Met His Companion

The faint glow of the west, the pomp of the then lonely woods of Richmond, were before us, behind and about us the darkening room, and on the stony face of the sufferer—for the character of his face, though still gentle and sweet, was changed—rested that dim, odd glow which seems to descend and produce, where it touches, lights, sudden though faint, which are lost, almost without gradation, in darkness. The silence, too, was utter: not a distant wheel, or bark, or whistle from without; and within the depressing stillness of an invalid bachelor's house.

I guessed well the nature, though not even vaguely the particulars of the revelations I was about to receive, from that fixed face of suffering that so oddly flushed stood out, like a portrait of Schalken's, before its background of darkness.

"It began," he said, "on the 15th of October, three years and eleven weeks ago, and two days—I keep very accurate count, for every day is torment. If I leave anywhere a chasm in my narrative tell me.

"About four years ago I began a work, which had cost me very much thought and reading. It was upon the religious metaphysics of the ancients."

"I know," said I, "the actual religion of educated and thinking paganism, quite apart from symbolic worship? A wide and very interesting field."

"Yes, but not good for the mind—the Christian mind, I mean. Paganism is all bound together in essential unity, and, with evil sympathy, their religion involves their art, and both their manners, and the subject is a degrading fascination and the Nemesis sure. God forgive me!

"I wrote a great deal; I wrote late at night. I was always thinking on the subject, walking about, wherever I was, everywhere. It thoroughly infected me. You are to remember that all the material ideas connected with it were more or less of the beautiful, the subject itself delightfully interesting, and I, then, without a care."

He sighed heavily.

"I believe, that every one who sets about writing in earnest does his work, as a friend of mine phrased it, on something—tea, or coffee, or tobacco. I suppose there is a material waste that must be hourly supplied in such occupations, or that we should grow too abstracted, and the mind, as it were, pass out of the body, unless it were reminded often enough of the connection by actual sensation. At all events, I felt the want, and I supplied it. Tea was my companion—at first the ordinary black tea, made in the usual way, not too strong: but I drank a good deal, and increased its strength as I went on. I never experienced an uncomfortable symptom from it. I began to take a little green tea. I found the effect pleasanter, it cleared and intensified the power of thought so, I had come to take it frequently, but not stronger than one might take it for pleasure. I wrote a great deal out here, it was so quiet, and in this room. I used to sit up very late, and it became a habit with me to sip my tea—green tea—every now and then as my work proceeded. I had a little kettle on my table, that swung over a lamp, and made tea two or three times between eleven o'clock and two or three in the morning, my hours of going to bed. I used to go into town every day. I was not a monk, and, although I spent an hour or two in a library, hunting up authorities and looking out lights upon my theme, I was in no morbid state as far as I can judge. I met my friends pretty much as usual and enjoyed their society, and, on the whole, existence had never been, I think, so pleasant before.

"I had met with a man who had some odd old books, German editions in mediaeval Latin, and I was only too happy to be permitted access to them. This obliging person's books were in the City, a very out-of-the-way part of it. I had rather out-stayed my intended hour, and, on coming out, seeing no cab near, I was tempted to get into the omnibus which used to drive past this house. It was darker than this by the time the 'bus had reached an old house, you may have remarked, with four poplars at each side of the door, and there the last passenger but myself got out. We drove along rather faster. It was twilight now. I leaned back in my corner next the door ruminating pleasantly.

"The interior of the omnibus was nearly dark. I had observed in the corner opposite to me at the other side, and at the end next the horses, two small circular reflections, as it seemed to me of a reddish light. They were about two inches apart, and about the size of those small brass buttons that yachting men used to put upon their jackets. I began to speculate, as listless men will, upon this trifle, as it seemed. From what centre did that faint but deep red light come, and from what—glass beads, buttons, toy decorations—was it reflected? We were lumbering along gently, having nearly a mile still to go. I had not solved the puzzle, and it became in another minute more odd, for these two luminous points, with a sudden jerk, descended nearer and nearer the floor, keeping still their relative distance and horizontal position, and then, as suddenly, they rose to the level of the seat on which I was sitting and I saw them no more.

"My curiosity was now really excited, and, before I had time to think, I saw again these two dull lamps, again together near the floor; again they disappeared, and again in their old corner I saw them.

"So, keeping my eyes upon them, I edged quietly up my own side, towards the end at which I still saw these tiny discs of red.

"There was very little light in the 'bus. It was nearly dark. I leaned forward to aid my endeavour to discover what these little circles really were. They shifted position a little as I did so. I began now to perceive an outline of something black, and I soon saw, with tolerable distinctness, the outline of a small black monkey, pushing its face forward in mimicry to meet mine; those were its eyes, and I now dimly saw its teeth grinning at me.

"I drew back, not knowing whether it might not meditate a spring. I fancied that one of the passengers had forgot this ugly pet, and wishing to ascertain something of its temper, though not caring to trust my fingers to it, I poked my umbrella softly towards it. It remained immovable—up to it—through it. For through it, and back and forward it passed, without the slightest resistance.

"I can't, in the least, convey to you the kind of horror that I felt. When I had ascertained that the thing was an illusion, as I then supposed, there came a misgiving about myself and a terror that fascinated me in impotence to remove my gaze from the eyes of the brute for some moments. As I looked, it made a little skip back, quite into the corner, and I, in a panic, found myself at the door, having put my head out, drawing deep breaths of the outer air, and staring at the lights and tress we were passing, too glad to reassure myself of reality.

"I stopped the 'bus and got out. I perceived the man look oddly at me as I paid him. I dare say there was something unusual in my looks and manner, for I had never felt so strangely before."

CHAPTER - VII

The Journey: First Stage

"**W**hen the omnibus drove on, and I was alone upon the road, I looked carefully round to ascertain whether the monkey had followed me. To my indescribable relief I saw it nowhere. I can't describe easily what a shock I had received, and my sense of genuine gratitude on finding myself, as I supposed, quite rid of it.

"I had got out a little before we reached this house, two or three hundred steps. A brick wall runs along the footpath, and inside the wall is a hedge of yew, or some dark evergreen of that kind, and within that again the row of fine trees which you may have remarked as you came.

"This brick wall is about as high as my shoulder, and happening to raise my eyes I saw the monkey, with that stooping gait, on all fours, walking or creeping, close beside me, on top of the wall. I stopped, looking at it with a feeling of loathing and horror. As I stopped so did it. It sat up on the wall with its long hands on its knees looking at me. There was not light enough to see it much more than in outline, nor was it dark enough to bring the peculiar light of its eyes into strong relief. I still saw, however, that red foggy light plainly enough. It did not show its teeth, nor exhibit any sign of irritation, but seemed jaded and sulky, and was observing me steadily.

"I drew back into the middle of the road. It was an unconscious recoil, and there I stood, still looking at it. It did not move.

"With an instinctive determination to try something—anything, I turned about and walked briskly towards town with askance look, all the time, watching the movements of the beast. It crept swiftly along the wall, at exactly my pace.

"Where the wall ends, near the turn of the road, it came down, and with a wiry spring or two brought itself close to my feet, and continued to keep

        GREEN TEA

up with me, as I quickened my pace. It was at my left side, so close to my leg that I felt every moment as if I should tread upon it.

"The road was quite deserted and silent, and it was darker every moment. I stopped dismayed and bewildered, turning as I did so, the other way—I mean, towards this house, away from which I had been walking. When I stood still, the monkey drew back to a distance of, I suppose, about five or six yards, and remained stationary, watching me.

"I had been more agitated than I have said. I had read, of course, as everyone has, something about 'spectral illusions,' as you physicians term the phenomena of such cases. I considered my situation, and looked my misfortune in the face.

"These affections, I had read, are sometimes transitory and sometimes obstinate. I had read of cases in which the appearance, at first harmless, had, step by step, degenerated into something direful and insupportable, and ended by wearing its victim out. Still as I stood there, but for my bestial companion, quite alone, I tried to comfort myself by repeating again and again the assurance, 'the thing is purely disease, a well-known physical affection, as distinctly as small-pox or neuralgia. Doctors are all agreed on that, philosophy demonstrates it. I must not be a fool. I've been sitting up too late, and I daresay my digestion is quite wrong, and, with God's help, I shall be all right, and this is but a symptom of nervous dyspepsia.' Did I believe all this? Not one word of it, no more than any other miserable being ever did who is once seized and riveted in this satanic captivity. Against my convictions, I might say my knowledge, I was simply bullying myself into a false courage.

"I now walked homeward. I had only a few hundred yards to go. I had forced myself into a sort of resignation, but I had not got over the sickening shock and the flurry of the first certainty of my misfortune.

"I made up my mind to pass the night at home. The brute moved close beside me, and I fancied there was the sort of anxious drawing toward the house, which one sees in tired horses or dogs, sometimes as they come toward home.

"I was afraid to go into town, I was afraid of any one's seeing and recognizing me. I was conscious of an irrepressible agitation in my manner. Also, I was afraid of any violent change in my habits, such as going to a place of amusement, or walking from home in order to fatigue myself. At the hall door it waited till I mounted the steps, and when the door was opened entered with me.

"I drank no tea that night. I got cigars and some brandy and water. My idea was that I should act upon my material system, and by living for a while in sensation apart from thought, send myself forcibly, as it were, into a new groove. I came up here to this drawing-room. I sat just here. The monkey then got upon a small table that then stood there. It looked dazed and languid. An irrepressible uneasiness as to its movements kept my eyes always upon it. Its eyes were half closed, but I could see them glow. It was looking steadily at me. In all situations, at all hours, it is awake and looking at me. That never changes.

"I shall not continue in detail my narrative of this particular night. I shall describe, rather, the phenomena of the first year, which never varied, essentially. I shall describe the monkey as it appeared in daylight. In the dark, as you shall presently hear, there are peculiarities. It is a small monkey, perfectly black. It had only one peculiarity—a character of malignity—unfathomable malignity. During the first year it looked sullen and sick. But this character of intense malice and vigilance was always underlying that surly languor. During all that time it acted as if on a plan of giving me as little trouble as was consistent with watching me. Its eyes were never off me. I have never lost sight of it, except in my sleep, light or dark, day or night, since it came here, excepting when it withdraws for some weeks at a time, unaccountably.

"In total dark it is visible as in daylight. I do not mean merely its eyes. It is all visible distinctly in a halo that resembles a glow of red embers, and which accompanies it in all its movements.

"When it leaves me for a time, it is always at night, in the dark, and in the same way. It grows at first uneasy, and then furious, and then advances towards me, grinning and shaking, its paws clenched, and, at the same time, there comes the appearance of fire in the grate. I never have any fire. I can't sleep in the room where there is any, and it draws nearer and nearer to the chimney, quivering, it seems, with rage, and when its fury rises to the highest pitch, it springs into the grate, and up the chimney, and I see it no more.

"When first this happened, I thought I was released. I was now a new man. A day passed—a night—and no return, and a blessed week—a week—another week. I was always on my knees, Dr. Hesselius, always, thanking God and praying. A whole month passed of liberty, but on a sudden, it was with me again."

　　　　　Green Tea

CHAPTER - VIII

The Second Stage

"It was with me, and the malice which before was torpid under a sullen exterior, was now active. It was perfectly unchanged in every other respect. This new energy was apparent in its activity and its looks, and soon in other ways.

"For a time, you will understand, the change was shown only in an increased vivacity, and an air of menace, as if it were always brooding over some atrocious plan. Its eyes, as before, were never off me."

"Is it here now?" I asked.

"No," he replied, "it has been absent exactly a fortnight and a day—fifteen days. It has sometimes been away so long as nearly two months, once for three. Its absence always exceeds a fortnight, although it may be but by a single day. Fifteen days having past since I saw it last, it may return now at any moment."

"Is its return," I asked, "accompanied by any peculiar manifestation?"

"Nothing—no," he said. "It is simply with me again. On lifting my eyes from a book, or turning my head, I see it, as usual, looking at me, and then it remains, as before, for its appointed time. I have never told so much and so minutely before to any one."

I perceived that he was agitated, and looking like death, and he repeatedly applied his handkerchief to his forehead; I suggested that he might be tired, and told him that I would call, with pleasure, in the morning, but he said:

"No, if you don't mind hearing it all now. I have got so far, and I should prefer making one effort of it. When I spoke to Dr. Harley, I had nothing like so much to tell. You are a philosophic physician. You give spirit its proper rank. If this thing is real—"

He paused looking at me with agitated inquiry.

"We can discuss it by-and-by, and very fully. I will give you all I think," I answered, after an interval.

"Well—very well. If it is anything real, I say, it is prevailing, little by little, and drawing me more interiorly into hell. Optic nerves, he talked of. Ah! well—there are other nerves of communication. May God Almighty help me! You shall hear.

"Its power of action, I tell you, had increased. Its malice became, in a way, aggressive. About two years ago, some questions that were pending between me and the bishop having been settled, I went down to my parish in Warwickshire, anxious to find occupation in my profession. I was not prepared for what happened, although I have since thought I might have apprehended something like it. The reason of my saying so is this—"

He was beginning to speak with a great deal more effort and reluctance, and sighed often, and seemed at times nearly overcome. But at this time his manner was not agitated. It was more like that of a sinking patient, who has given himself up.

"Yes, but I will first tell you about Kenlis, my parish.

"It was with me when I left this place for Dawlbridge. It was my silent travelling companion, and it remained with me at the vicarage. When I entered on the discharge of my duties, another change took place. The thing exhibited an atrocious determination to thwart me. It was with me in the church—in the reading-desk—in the pulpit—within the communion rails. At last, it reached this extremity, that while I was reading to the congregation, it would spring upon the book and squat there, so that I was unable to see the page. This happened more than once.

"I left Dawlbridge for a time. I placed myself in Dr. Harley's hands. I did everything he told me. He gave my case a great deal of thought. It interested him, I think. He seemed successful. For nearly three months I was perfectly free from a return. I began to think I was safe. With his full assent I returned to Dawlbridge.

"I travelled in a chaise. I was in good spirits. I was more—I was happy and grateful. I was returning, as I thought, delivered from a dreadful hallucination, to the scene of duties which I longed to enter upon. It was a beautiful sunny evening, everything looked serene and cheerful, and I was delighted. I remember looking out of the window to see the spire of my church at Kenlis among the trees, at the point where one has the earliest view of it. It is exactly where the little stream that bounds the parish passes under the road by a culvert, and where it emerges at the road-side, a stone with an old inscription is placed. As we passed this point, I drew my head in and sat down, and in the corner of the chaise was the monkey.

"For a moment I felt faint, and then quite wild with despair and horror. I called to the driver, and got out, and sat down at the road-side, and prayed to God silently for mercy. A despairing resignation supervened. My companion was with me as I re-entered the vicarage. The same persecution followed. After a short struggle I submitted, and soon I left the place.

"I told you," he said, "that the beast has before this become in certain ways aggressive. I will explain a little. It seemed to be actuated by intense and increasing fury, whenever I said my prayers, or even meditated prayer. It amounted at last to a dreadful interruption. You will ask, how could a silent immaterial phantom effect that? It was thus, whenever I meditated praying; It was always before me, and nearer and nearer.

"It used to spring on a table, on the back of a chair, on the chimney-piece, and slowly to swing itself from side to side, looking at me all the time. There is in its motion an indefinable power to dissipate thought, and to contract one's attention to that monotony, till the ideas shrink, as it were, to a point, and at last to nothing—and unless I had started up, and shook off the catalepsy I have felt as if my mind were on the point of losing itself. There are other ways," he sighed heavily; "thus, for instance, while I pray with my eyes closed, it comes closer and closer, and I see it. I know it is not to be accounted for physically, but I do actually see it, though my lids are dosed, and so it rocks my mind, as it were, and overpowers me, and I am obliged to rise from my knees. If you had ever yourself known this, you would be acquainted with desperation."

CHAPTER - IX

The Third Stage

"I see, Dr. Hesselius, that you don't lose one word of my statement. I need not ask you to listen specially to what I am now going to tell you. They talk of the optic nerves, and of spectral illusions, as if the organ of sight was the only point assailable by the influences that have fastened upon me—I know better. For two years in my direful case that limitation prevailed. But as food is taken in softly at the lips, and then brought under the teeth, as the tip of the little finger caught in a mill crank will draw in the hand, and the arm, and the whole body, so the miserable mortal who has been once caught firmly by the end of the finest fibre of his nerve, is drawn in and in, by the enormous machinery of hell, until he is as I am. Yes, Doctor, as I am, for a while I talk to you, and implore relief, I feel that my prayer is for the impossible, and my pleading with the inexorable."

I endeavoured to calm his visibly increasing agitation, and told him that he must not despair.

While we talked the night had overtaken us. The filmy moonlight was wide over the scene which the window commanded, and I said:

"Perhaps you would prefer having candles. This light, you know, is odd. I should wish you, as much as possible, under your usual conditions while I make my diagnosis, shall I call it—otherwise I don't care."

"All lights are the same to me," he said; "except when I read or write, I care not if night were perpetual. I am going to tell you what happened about a year ago. The thing began to speak to me."

"Speak! How do you mean—speak as a man does, do you mean?"

"Yes; speak in words and consecutive sentences, with perfect coherence and articulation; but there is a peculiarity. It is not like the tone of a human voice. It is not by my ears it reaches me—it comes like a singing through my head.

"This faculty, the power of speaking to me, will be my undoing. It won't let me pray, it interrupts me with dreadful blasphemies. I dare not go on, I could not. Oh! Doctor, can the skill, and thought, and prayers of man avail me nothing!"

"You must promise me, my dear sir, not to trouble yourself with unnecessarily exciting thoughts; confine yourself strictly to the narrative of facts; and recollect, above all, that even if the thing that infests you be, you seem to suppose a reality with an actual independent life and will, yet it can have no power to hurt you, unless it be given from above: its access to your senses depends mainly upon your physical condition—this is, under God, your comfort and reliance: we are all alike environed. It is only that in your case, the 'paries,' the veil of the flesh, the screen, is a little out of repair, and sights and sounds are transmitted. We must enter on a new course, sir,—be encouraged. I'll give to-night to the careful consideration of the whole case."

"You are very good, sir; you think it worth trying, you don't give me quite up; but, sir, you don't know, it is gaining such an influence over me: it orders me about, it is such a tyrant, and I'm growing so helpless. May God deliver me!"

"It orders you about—of course you mean by speech?"

"Yes, yes; it is always urging me to crimes, to injure others, or myself. You see, Doctor, the situation is urgent, it is indeed. When I was in Shropshire, a few weeks ago" (Mr. Jennings was speaking rapidly and trembling now, holding my arm with one hand, and looking in my face), "I went out one day with a party of friends for a walk: my persecutor, I tell you, was with me at the time. I lagged behind the rest: the country near the Dee, you know, is beautiful. Our path happened to lie near a coal mine, and at the verge of the wood is a perpendicular shaft, they say, a hundred and fifty feet deep. My niece had remained behind with me—she knows, of course nothing of the nature of my sufferings. She knew, however, that I had been ill, and was low, and she remained to prevent my being quite alone. As we loitered slowly on together, the brute that accompanied me was urging me to throw myself down the shaft. I tell you now—oh, sir, think of it!—the one consideration that saved me from that hideous death was the fear lest the shock of witnessing the occurrence should be too much for the poor girl. I asked her to go on and walk with her friends, saying that I could go no further. She made excuses, and the more I urged her the firmer she became. She looked doubtful and frightened. I suppose there was something in my looks or manner that alarmed her; but she would not go, and that literally saved me. You had no idea, sir, that a living man could be made so abject a slave of Satan," he said, with a ghastly groan and a shudder.

There was a pause here, and I said, "You were preserved nevertheless. It was the act of God. You are in His hands and in the power of no other being: be therefore confident for the future."

CHAPTER - X

Home

Imade him have candles lighted, and saw the room looking cheery and inhabited before I left him. I told him that he must regard his illness strictly as one dependent on physical, though subtle physical causes. I told him that he had evidence of God's care and love in the deliverance which he had just described, and that I had perceived with pain that he seemed to regard its peculiar features as indicating that he had been delivered over to spiritual reprobation. Than such a conclusion nothing could be, I insisted, less warranted; and not only so, but more contrary to facts, as disclosed in his mysterious deliverance from that murderous influence during his Shropshire excursion. First, his niece had been retained by his side without his intending to keep her near him; and, secondly, there had been infused into his mind an irresistible repugnance to execute the dreadful suggestion in her presence.

As I reasoned this point with him, Mr. Jennings wept. He seemed comforted. One promise I exacted, which was that should the monkey at any time return, I should be sent for immediately; and, repeating my assurance that I would give neither time nor thought to any other subject until I had thoroughly investigated his case, and that to-morrow he should hear the result, I took my leave.

Before getting into the carriage I told the servant that his master was far from well, and that he should make a point of frequently looking into his room. My own arrangements I made with a view to being quite secure from interruption.

I merely called at my lodgings, and with a travelling-desk and carpet-bag, set off in a hackney carriage for an inn about two miles out of town, called "The Horns," a very quiet and comfortable house, with good thick walls.

And there I resolved, without the possibility of intrusion or distraction, to devote some hours of the night, in my comfortable sitting-room, to Mr. Jennings' case, and so much of the morning as it might require.

(There occurs here a careful note of Dr. Hesselius' opinion upon the case, and of the habits, dietary, and medicines which he prescribed. It is curious—some persons would say mystical. But, on the whole, I doubt whether it would sufficiently interest a reader of the kind I am likely to meet with, to warrant its being here reprinted. The whole letter was plainly written at the inn where he had hid himself for the occasion. The next letter is dated from his town lodgings.)

I left town for the inn where I slept last night at half-past nine, and did not arrive at my room in town until one o'clock this afternoon. I found a letter in Mr. Jennings' hand upon my table. It had not come by post, and, on inquiry, I learned that Mr. Jennings' servant had brought it, and on learning that I was not to return until to-day, and that no one could tell him my address, he seemed very uncomfortable, and said his orders from his master were that that he was not to return without an answer.

I opened the letter and read:

DEAR DR. HESSELIUS.—It is here. You had not been an hour gone when it returned. It is speaking. It knows all that has happened. It knows everything—it knows you, and is frantic and atrocious. It reviles. I send you this. It knows every word I have written—I write. This I promised, and I therefore write, but I fear very confused, very incoherently. I am so interrupted, disturbed.

Ever yours, sincerely yours,

Robert Lynder Jennings.

"When did this come?" I asked.

"About eleven last night: the man was here again, and has been here three times to-day. The last time is about an hour since."

Thus answered, and with the notes I had made upon his case in my pocket, I was in a few minutes driving towards Richmond, to see Mr. Jennings.

I by no means, as you perceive, despaired of Mr. Jennings' case. He had himself remembered and applied, though quite in a mistaken way, the principle which I lay down in my Metaphysical Medicine, and which governs all such cases. I was about to apply it in earnest. I was profoundly interested, and very anxious to see and examine him while the "enemy" was actually present.

I drove up to the sombre house, and ran up the steps, and knocked. The door, in a little time, was opened by a tall woman in black silk. She looked ill, and as if she had been crying. She curtseyed, and heard my question, but she did not answer. She turned her face away, extending her hand towards two men who were coming down-stairs; and thus having, as it were, tacitly made me over to them, she passed through a side-door hastily and shut it.

The man who was nearest the hall, I at once accosted, but being now close to him, I was shocked to see that both his hands were covered with blood.

I drew back a little, and the man, passing downstairs, merely said in a low tone, "Here's the servant, sir."

The servant had stopped on the stairs, confounded and dumb at seeing me. He was rubbing his hands in a handkerchief, and it was steeped in blood.

"Jones, what is it? what has happened?" I asked, while a sickening suspicion overpowered me.

The man asked me to come up to the lobby. I was beside him in a moment, and, frowning and pallid, with contracted eyes, he told me the horror which I already half guessed.

His master had made away with himself.

I went upstairs with him to the room—what I saw there I won't tell you. He had cut his throat with his razor. It was a frightful gash. The two men had laid him on the bed, and composed his limbs. It had happened, as the immense pool of blood on the floor declared, at some distance between the bed and the window. There was carpet round his bed, and a carpet under his dressing-table, but none on the rest of the floor, for the man said he did not like a carpet on his bedroom. In this sombre and now terrible room, one of the great elms that darkened the house was slowly moving the shadow of one of its great boughs upon this dreadful floor.

I beckoned to the servant, and we went downstairs together. I turned off the hall into an old-fashioned panelled room, and there standing, I heard all the servant had to tell. It was not a great deal.

"I concluded, sir, from your words, and looks, sir, as you left last night, that you thought my master was seriously ill. I thought it might be that you were afraid of a fit, or something. So I attended very close to your directions. He sat up late, till past three o'clock. He was not writing or reading. He was talking a great deal to himself, but that was nothing unusual. At about that hour I assisted him to undress, and left him in his slippers and dressing-gown. I went back softly in about half-an-hour. He was in his bed, quite undressed, and a pair of candles lighted on the table beside his bed. He was leaning on his elbow, and looking out at the other side of the bed when I came in. I asked him if he wanted anything, and he said No.

"I don't know whether it was what you said to me, sir, or something a little unusual about him, but I was uneasy, uncommon uneasy about him last night.

"In another half hour, or it might be a little more, I went up again. I did not hear him talking as before. I opened the door a little. The candles were both out, which was not usual. I had a bedroom candle, and I let the light in, a little bit, looking softly round. I saw him sitting in that chair beside the dressing-table with his clothes on again. He turned round and looked at me. I thought it strange he should get up and dress, and put out the candles to sit in the dark, that way. But I only asked him again if I could do anything for him. He said, No, rather sharp, I thought. I asked him if I might light the candles, and he said, 'Do as you like, Jones.' So I lighted them, and I lingered about the room, and he said, 'Tell me truth, Jones; why did you come again—you did not hear anyone cursing?' 'No, sir,' I said, wondering what he could mean.

"'No,' said he, after me, 'of course, no;' and I said to him, 'Wouldn't it be well, sir, you went to bed? It's just five o'clock;' and he said nothing, but, 'Very likely; good-night, Jones.' So I went, sir, but in less than an hour I came again. The door was fast, and he heard me, and called as I thought from the bed to know what I wanted, and he desired me not to disturb him again. I lay down and slept for a little. It must have been between six and seven when I went up again. The door was still fast, and he made no answer, so I did not like to disturb him, and thinking he was asleep, I left him till nine. It was his custom to ring when he wished me to come, and I had no particular hour for calling him. I tapped very gently, and getting no answer, I stayed away a good while, supposing he was getting some rest then. It was not till eleven o'clock I grew really uncomfortable about him— for at the latest he was never, that I could remember, later than half-past ten. I got no answer. I knocked and called, and still no answer. So not being able to force the door, I called Thomas from the stables, and together we forced it, and found him in the shocking way you saw."

Jones had no more to tell. Poor Mr. Jennings was very gentle, and very kind. All his people were fond of him. I could see that the servant was very much moved.

So, dejected and agitated, I passed from that terrible house, and its dark canopy of elms, and I hope I shall never see it more. While I write to you I feel like a man who has but half waked from a frightful and monotonous dream. My memory rejects the picture with incredulity and horror. Yet I know it is true. It is the story of the process of a poison, a poison which excites the reciprocal action of spirit and nerve, and paralyses the tissue that separates those cognate functions of the senses, the external and the interior. Thus we find strange bed-fellows, and the mortal and immortal prematurely make acquaintance.

CONCLUSION

A Word for Those Who Suffer

My dear Van L——, you have suffered from an affection similar to that which I have just described. You twice complained of a return of it.

Who, under God, cured you? Your humble servant, Martin Hesselius. Let me rather adopt the more emphasised piety of a certain good old French surgeon of three hundred years ago: "I treated, and God cured you."

Come, my friend, you are not to be hippish. Let me tell you a fact.

I have met with, and treated, as my book shows, fifty-seven cases of this kind of vision, which I term indifferently "sublimated," "precocious," and "interior."

There is another class of affections which are truly termed—though commonly confounded with those which I describe—spectral illusions. These latter I look upon as being no less simply curable than a cold in the head or a trifling dyspepsia.

It is those which rank in the first category that test our promptitude of thought. Fifty-seven such cases have I encountered, neither more nor less. And in how many of these have I failed? In no one single instance.

There is no one affliction of mortality more easily and certainly reducible, with a little patience, and a rational confidence in the physician. With these simple conditions, I look upon the cure as absolutely certain.

You are to remember that I had not even commenced to treat Mr. Jennings' case. I have not any doubt that I should have cured him perfectly in eighteen months, or possibly it might have extended to two years. Some cases are very rapidly curable, others extremely tedious. Every intelligent physician who will give thought and diligence to the task, will effect a cure.

You know my tract on "The Cardinal Functions of the Brain." I there, by the evidence of innumerable facts, prove, as I think, the high probability of a circulation arterial and venous in its mechanism, through the nerves. Of this system, thus considered, the brain is the heart. The fluid, which is propagated hence through one class of nerves, returns in an altered state through another, and the nature of that fluid is spiritual, though not immaterial, any more than, as I before remarked, light or electricity are so.

By various abuses, among which the habitual use of such agents as green tea is one, this fluid may be affected as to its quality, but it is more frequently disturbed as to equilibrium. This fluid being that which we have in common with spirits, a congestion found upon the masses of brain or nerve, connected with the interior sense, forms a surface unduly exposed, on which disembodied spirits may operate: communication is thus more or less effectually established. Between this brain circulation and the heart circulation there is an intimate sympathy. The seat, or rather the instrument of exterior vision, is the eye. The seat of interior vision is the nervous tissue and brain, immediately about and above the eyebrow. You remember how effectually I dissipated your pictures by the simple application of iced eau-de-cologne. Few cases, however, can be treated exactly alike with anything like rapid success. Cold acts powerfully as a repellant of the nervous fluid. Long enough continued it will even produce that permanent insensibility which we call numbness, and a little longer, muscular as well as sensational paralysis.

I have not, I repeat, the slightest doubt that I should have first dimmed and ultimately sealed that inner eye which Mr. Jennings had inadvertently opened. The same senses are opened in delirium tremens, and entirely shut up again when the overaction of the cerebral heart, and the prodigious nervous congestions that attend it, are terminated by a decided change in the state of the body. It is by acting steadily upon the body, by a simple process, that this result is produced—and inevitably produced—I have never yet failed.

Poor Mr. Jennings made away with himself. But that catastrophe was the result of a totally different malady, which, as it were, projected itself upon the disease which was established. His case was in the distinctive manner a complication, and the complaint under which he really succumbed, was hereditary suicidal mania. Poor Mr. Jennings I cannot call a patient of mine, for I had not even begun to treat his case, and he had not yet given me, I am convinced, his full and unreserved confidence. If the patient do not array himself on the side of the disease, his cure is certain.

MR. JUSTICE HARBOTTLE

❖

PROLOGUE

On this case Doctor Hesselius has inscribed nothing more than the words, "Harman's Report," and a simple reference to his own extraordinary Essay on "The Interior Sense, and the Conditions of the Opening thereof."

The reference is to Vol. I., Section 317, Note ZA. The note to which reference is thus made, simply says: "There are two accounts of the remarkable case of the Honourable Mr. Justice Harbottle, one furnished to me by Mrs. Trimmer, of Tunbridge Wells (June, 1805); the other at a much later date, by Anthony Harman, Esq. I much prefer the former; in the first place, because it is minute and detailed, and written, it seems to me, with more caution and knowledge; and in the next, because the letters from Dr. Hedstone, which are embodied in it, furnish matter of the highest value to a right apprehension of the nature of the case. It was one of the best declared cases of an opening of the interior sense, which I have met with. It was affected too, by the phenomenon, which occurs so frequently as to indicate a law of these eccentric conditions; that is to say, it exhibited what I may term, the contagious character of this sort of intrusion of the spirit-world upon the proper domain of matter. So soon as the spirit-action has established itself in the case of one patient, its developed energy begins to radiate, more or less effectually, upon others. The interior vision of the child was opened; as was, also, that of its mother, Mrs. Pyneweck; and both the interior vision and hearing of the scullery-maid, were opened on the same occasion. After-appearances are the result of the law explained in Vol. II., Section 17 to 49. The common centre of association, simultaneously recalled, unites, or reunites, as the case may be, for a period measured, as we see, in Section 37. The maximum will extend to days, the minimum is little more than a second. We see the operation of this principle perfectly displayed, in certain cases of lunacy, of epilepsy, of catalepsy, and of mania, of a peculiar and painful character, though unattended by incapacity of business."

The memorandum of the case of Judge Harbottle, which was written by Mrs. Trimmer, of Tunbridge Wells, which Doctor Hesselius thought the better of the two, I have been unable to discover among his papers. I found in his escritoire a note to the effect that he had lent the Report of Judge Harbottle's case, written by Mrs. Trimmer, to Dr. F. Heyne. To that learned and able gentleman accordingly I wrote, and received from him, in his reply, which was full of alarms and regrets, on account of the uncertain safety of that "valuable MS.," a line written long since by Dr. Hesselius, which completely exonerated him, inasmuch as it acknowledged the safe return of the papers. The narrative of Mr. Harman, is therefore, the only one available for this collection. The late Dr. Hesselius, in another passage of the note that I have cited, says, "As to the facts (non-medical) of the case, the narrative of Mr. Harman exactly tallies with that furnished by Mrs. Trimmer." The strictly scientific view of the case would scarcely interest the popular reader; and, possibly, for the purposes of this selection, I should, even had I both papers to choose between, have preferred that of Mr. Harman, which is given, in full, in the following pages.

CHAPTER - I

The Judge's House

Thirty years ago, an elderly man, to whom I paid quarterly a small annuity charged on some property of mine, came on the quarter-day to receive it. He was a dry, sad, quiet man, who had known better days, and had always maintained an unexceptionable character. No better authority could be imagined for a ghost story.

He told me one, though with a manifest reluctance; he was drawn into the narration by his choosing to explain what I should not have remarked, that he had called two days earlier than that week after the strict day of payment, which he had usually allowed to elapse. His reason was a sudden determination to change his lodgings, and the consequent necessity of paying his rent a little before it was due.

He lodged in a dark street in Westminster, in a spacious old house, very warm, being wainscoted from top to bottom, and furnished with no undue abundance of windows, and those fitted with thick sashes and small panes.

This house was, as the bills upon the windows testified, offered to be sold or let. But no one seemed to care to look at it.

A thin matron, in rusty black silk, very taciturn, with large, steady, alarmed eyes, that seemed to look in your face, to read what you might have seen in the dark rooms and passages through which you had passed, was in charge of it, with a solitary "maid-of-all-work" under her command. My poor friend had taken lodgings in this house, on account of their extraordinary cheapness. He had occupied them for nearly a year without the slightest disturbance, and was the only tenant, under rent, in the house. He had two rooms; a sitting-room and a bed-room with a closet opening from it, in which he kept his books and papers locked up. He had gone to his bed, having also locked the outer door. Unable to sleep, he had lighted a candle, and after having read for a time, had laid the book beside him. He heard the old clock at the stairhead strike one; and very shortly after, to his alarm, he saw the closet-door, which he thought he had locked, open stealthily, and a slight dark man, particularly sinister, and somewhere about fifty, dressed in mourning of a very antique fashion, such a suit as we see in Hogarth, entered the room on tip-toe. He was followed by an elder man, stout, and blotched with scurvy, and whose features, fixed as a corpse's, were stamped with dreadful force with a character of sensuality and villany.

This old man wore a flowered silk dressing-gown and ruffles, and he remarked a gold ring on his finger, and on his head a cap of velvet, such as, in the days of perukes, gentlemen wore in undress.

This direful old man carried in his ringed and ruffled hand a coil of rope; and these two figures crossed the floor diagonally, passing the foot of his bed, from the closet door at the farther end of the room, at the left, near the window, to the door opening upon the lobby, close to the bed's head, at his right.

"These Two Figures Crossed the Floor Diagonally, Passing The Foot of the Bed."

He did not attempt to describe his sensations as these figures passed so near him. He merely said, that so far from sleeping in that room again, no consideration the world could offer would induce him so much as to enter it again alone, even in the daylight. He found both doors, that of the closet, and that of the room opening upon the lobby, in the morning fast locked as he had left them before going to bed.

In answer to a question of mine, he said that neither appeared the least conscious of his presence. They did not seem to glide, but walked as living men do, but without any sound, and he felt a vibration on the floor as they crossed it. He so obviously suffered from speaking about the apparitions, that I asked him no more questions.

There were in his description, however, certain coincidences so very singular, as to induce me, by that very post, to write to a friend much my senior, then living in a remote part of England, for the information which I knew he could give me. He had himself more than once pointed out that old house to my attention, and told me, though very briefly, the strange story which I now asked him to give me in greater detail.

His answer satisfied me; and the following pages convey its substance.

Your letter (he wrote) tells me you desire some particulars about the closing years of the life of Mr. Justice Harbottle, one of the judges of the Court of Common Pleas. You refer, of course, to the extraordinary occurrences that made that period of his life long after a theme for "winter tales" and metaphysical speculation. I happen to know perhaps more than any other man living of those mysterious particulars.

The old family mansion, when I revisited London, more than thirty years ago, I examined for the last time. During the years that have passed since then, I hear that improvement, with its preliminary demolitions, has been doing wonders for the quarter of Westminster in which it stood. If I were quite certain that the house had been taken down, I should have no difficulty about naming the street in which it stood. As what I have to tell, however, is not likely to improve its letting value, and as I should not care to get into trouble, I prefer being silent on that particular point.

How old the house was, I can't tell. People said it was built by Roger Harbottle, a Turkey merchant, in the reign of King James I. I am not a good opinion upon such questions; but having been in it, though in its forlorn and deserted state, I can tell you in a general way what it was like. It was built of dark-red brick, and the door and windows were faced with stone that had turned yellow by time. It receded some feet from the line of the other houses in the street; and it had a florid and fanciful rail of iron about the broad steps that invited your ascent to the hall-door, in which were fixed, under a file of lamps among scrolls and twisted leaves, two immense "extinguishers," like the conical caps of fairies, into which, in old times, the footmen used to thrust their flambeaux when their chairs or coaches had set down their great people, in the hall or at the steps, as the case might be. That hall is panelled up to the ceiling, and has a large fire-place. Two or three stately old rooms open from it at each side. The windows of these are tall, with many small panes. Passing through the arch at the back of the hall, you come upon the wide and heavy well-staircase. There is a back staircase also. The mansion is large, and has not as much light, by any means, in proportion to its extent, as modern houses enjoy. When I saw it, it had long been untenanted, and had the gloomy reputation beside of a haunted house. Cobwebs floated from the ceilings or spanned the corners of the cornices, and dust lay thick over everything. The windows were stained with the dust and rain of fifty years, and darkness had thus grown darker.

When I made it my first visit, it was in company with my father, when I was still a boy, in the year 1808. I was about twelve years old, and my imagination impressible, as it always is at that age. I looked about me with great awe. I was here in the very centre and scene of those occurrences which I had heard recounted at the fireside at home, with so delightful a horror.

My father was an old bachelor of nearly sixty when he married. He had, when a child, seen Judge Harbottle on the bench in his robes and wig a dozen times at least before his death, which took place in 1748, and his appearance made a powerful and unpleasant impression, not only on his imagination, but upon his nerves.

The Judge was at that time a man of some sixty-seven years. He had a great mulberry-coloured face, a big, carbuncled nose, fierce eyes, and a grim and brutal mouth. My father, who was young at the time, thought it the most formidable face he had ever seen; for there were evidences of intellectual power in the formation and lines of the forehead. His voice was loud and harsh, and gave effect to the sarcasm which was his habitual weapon on the bench.

This old gentleman had the reputation of being about the wickedest man in England. Even on the bench he now and then showed his scorn of opinion. He had carried cases his own way, it was said, in spite of counsel, authorities, and even of juries, by a sort of cajolery, violence, and bamboozling, that somehow confused and overpowered resistance. He had never actually committed himself; he was too cunning to do that. He had the character of being, however, a dangerous and unscrupulous judge; but his character did not trouble him. The associates he chose for his hours of relaxation cared as little as he did about it.

CHAPTER - II

Mr. Peters

One night during the session of 1746 this old Judge went down in his chair to wait in one of the rooms of the House of Lords for the result of a division in which he and his order were interested.

This over, he was about to return to his house close by, in his chair; but the night had become so soft and fine that he changed his mind, sent it home empty, and with two footmen, each with a flambeau, set out on foot in preference. Gout had made him rather a slow pedestrian. It took him some time to get through the two or three streets he had to pass before reaching his house.

In one of those narrow streets of tall houses, perfectly silent at that hour, he overtook, slowly as he was walking, a very singular-looking old gentleman.

He had a bottle-green coat on, with a cape to it, and large stone buttons, a broad-leafed low-crowned hat, from under which a big powdered wig escaped; he stooped very much, and supported his bending knees with the aid of a crutch-handled cane, and so shuffled and tottered along painfully.

"I ask your pardon, sir," said this old man, in a very quavering voice, as the burly Judge came up with him, and he extended his hand feebly towards his arm.

Mr. Justice Harbottle saw that the man was by no means poorly dressed, and his manner that of a gentleman.

The Judge stopped short, and said, in his harsh peremptory tones, "Well, sir, how can I serve you?"

"Can you direct me to Judge Harbottle's house? I have some intelligence of the very last importance to communicate to him."

"Can you tell it before witnesses?" asked the Judge.

"By no means; it must reach his ear only," quavered the old man earnestly.

"If that be so, sir, you have only to accompany me a few steps farther to reach my house, and obtain a private audience; for I am Judge Harbottle."

With this invitation the infirm gentleman in the white wig complied very readily; and in another minute the stranger stood in what was then termed the front parlour of the Judge's house, tête-à-tête with that shrewd and dangerous functionary.

He had to sit down, being very much exhausted, and unable for a little time to speak; and then he had a fit of coughing, and after that a fit of gasping; and thus two or three minutes passed, during which the Judge dropped his roquelaure on an arm-chair, and threw his cocked-hat over that.

The venerable pedestrian in the white wig quickly recovered his voice. With closed doors they remained together for some time.

There were guests waiting in the drawing-rooms, and the sound of men's voices laughing, and then of a female voice singing to a harpsichord, were heard distinctly in the hall over the stairs; for old Judge Harbottle had arranged one of his dubious jollifications, such as might well make the hair of godly men's heads stand upright for that night.

This old gentleman in the powdered white wig, that rested on his stooped shoulders, must have had something to say that interested the Judge very much; for he would not have parted on easy terms with the ten minutes and upwards which that conference filched from the sort of revelry in which he most delighted, and in which he was the roaring king, and in some sort the tyrant also, of his company.

The footman who showed the aged gentleman out observed that the Judge's mulberry-coloured face, pimples and all, were bleached to a dingy yellow, and there was the abstraction of agitated thought in his manner, as he bid the stranger good-night. The servant saw that the conversation had been of serious import, and that the Judge was frightened.

Instead of stumping upstairs forthwith to his scandalous hilarities, his profane company, and his great china bowl of punch—the identical bowl from which a bygone Bishop of London, good easy man, had baptised this Judge's grandfather, now clinking round the rim with silver ladles, and hung with scrolls of lemon-peel—instead, I say, of stumping and clambering up the great staircase to the cavern of his Circean enchantment, he stood with his big nose flattened against the window-pane, watching the progress of the feeble old man, who clung stiffly to the iron rail as he got down, step by step, to the pavement.

The hall-door had hardly closed, when the old Judge was in the hall bawling hasty orders, with such stimulating expletives as old colonels under excitement sometimes indulge in now-a-days, with a stamp or two of his big foot, and a waving of his clenched fist in the air. He commanded the footman to overtake the old gentleman in the white wig, to offer him his protection on his way home, and in no case to show his face again without having ascertained where he lodged, and who he was, and all about him.

"By ——, sirrah! if you fail me in this, you doff my livery to-night!"

Forth bounced the stalwart footman, with his heavy cane under his arm, and skipped down the steps, and looked up and down the street after the singular figure, so easy to recognize.

What were his adventures I shall not tell you just now.

The old man, in the conference to which he had been admitted in that stately panelled room, had just told the Judge a very strange story. He might be himself a conspirator; he might possibly be crazed; or possibly his whole story was straight and true.

The aged gentleman in the bottle-green coat, in finding himself alone with Mr. Justice Harbottle, had become agitated. He said,

"There is, perhaps you are not aware, my lord, a prisoner in Shrewsbury jail, charged with having forged a bill of exchange for a hundred and twenty pounds, and his name is Lewis Pyneweck, a grocer of that town."

"Is there?" says the Judge, who knew well that there was.

"Yes, my lord," says the old man.

"Then you had better say nothing to affect this case. If you do, by ——, I'll commit you! for I'm to try it," says the judge, with his terrible look and tone.

"I am not going to do anything of the kind, my lord; of him or his case I know nothing, and care nothing. But a fact has come to my knowledge which it behoves you to well consider."

"And what may that fact be?" inquired the Judge; "I'm in haste, sir, and beg you will use dispatch."

"It has come to my knowledge, my lord, that a secret tribunal is in process of formation, the object of which is to take cognisance of the conduct of the judges; and first, of your conduct, my lord; it is a wicked conspiracy."

"Who are of it?" demands the Judge.

"I know not a single name as yet. I know but the fact, my lord; it is most certainly true."

"I'll have you before the Privy Council, sir," says the Judge.

"That is what I most desire; but not for a day or two, my lord."

"And why so?"

"I have not as yet a single name, as I told your lordship; but I expect to have a list of the most forward men in it, and some other papers connected with the plot, in two or three days."

"You said one or two just now."

"About that time, my lord."

"Is this a Jacobite plot?"

"In the main I think it is, my lord."

"Why, then, it is political. I have tried no State prisoners, nor am like to try any such. How, then, doth it concern me?"

"From what I can gather, my lord, there are those in it who desire private revenges upon certain judges."

"What do they call their cabal?"

"The High Court of Appeal, my lord."

"Who are you, sir? What is your name?"

"Hugh Peters, my lord."

"That should be a Whig name?"

"It is, my lord." "Where do you lodge, Mr. Peters?"

"In Thames Street, my lord, over against the sign of the 'Three Kings.'"

"'Three Kings?' Take care one be not too many for you, Mr. Peters! How come you, an honest Whig, as you say, to be privy to a Jacobite plot? Answer me that."

"My lord, a person in whom I take an interest has been seduced to take a part in it; and being frightened at the unexpected wickedness of their plans, he is resolved to become an informer for the Crown."

"He resolves like a wise man, sir. What does he say of the persons? Who are in the plot? Doth he know them?"

"Only two, my lord; but he will be introduced to the club in a few days, and he will then have a list, and more exact information of their plans, and above all of their oaths, and their hours and places of meeting, with which he wishes to be acquainted before they can have any suspicions of his intentions. And being so informed, to whom, think you, my lord, had he best go then?"

"To the king's attorney-general straight. But you say this concerns me, sir, in particular? How about this prisoner, Lewis Pyneweck? Is he one of them?"

"I can't tell, my lord; but for some reason, it is thought your lordship will be well advised if you try him not. For if you do, it is feared 'twill shorten your days."

"So far as I can learn, Mr. Peters, this business smells pretty strong of blood and treason. The king's attorney-general will know how to deal with it. When shall I see you again, sir?"

"If you give me leave, my lord, either before your lordship's court sits, or after it rises, to-morrow. I should like to come and tell your lordship what has passed."

"Do so, Mr. Peters, at nine o'clock to-morrow morning. And see you play me no trick, sir, in this matter; if you do, by ——, sir, I'll lay you by the heels!"

"You need fear no trick from me, my lord; had I not wished to serve you, and acquit my own conscience, I never would have come all this way to talk with your lordship."

"I'm willing to believe you, Mr. Peters; I'm willing to believe you, sir."

And upon this they parted.

"He has either painted his face, or he is consumedly sick," thought the old Judge.

The light had shown more effectually upon his features as he turned to leave the room with a low bow, and they looked, he fancied, unnaturally chalky.

"D—— him!" said the Judge ungraciously, as he began to scale the stairs: "he has half-spoiled my supper."

But if he had, no one but the Judge himself perceived it, and the evidence was all, as any one might perceive, the other way.

CHAPTER - III

Lewis Pyneweck

In the meantime the footman dispatched in pursuit of Mr. Peters speedily overtook that feeble gentleman. The old man stopped when he heard the sound of pursuing steps, but any alarms that may have crossed his mind seemed to disappear on his recognizing the livery. He very gratefully accepted the proffered assistance, and placed his tremulous arm within the servant's for support. They had not gone far, however, when the old man stopped suddenly, saying,

"Dear me! as I live, I have dropped it. You heard it fall. My eyes, I fear, won't serve me, and I'm unable to stoop low enough; but if you will look, you shall have half the find. It is a guinea; I carried it in my glove."

The street was silent and deserted. The footman had hardly descended to what he termed his "hunkers," and begun to search the pavement about the spot which the old man indicated, when Mr. Peters, who seemed very much exhausted, and breathed with difficulty, struck him a violent blow, from above, over the back of the head with a heavy instrument, and then another; and leaving him bleeding and senseless in the gutter, ran like a lamplighter down a lane to the right, and was gone.

When an hour later, the watchman brought the man in livery home, still stupid and covered with blood, Judge Harbottle cursed his servant roundly, swore he was drunk, threatened him with an indictment for taking bribes to betray his master, and cheered him with a perspective of the broad street leading from the Old Bailey to Tyburn, the cart's tail, and the hangman's lash.

Notwithstanding this demonstration, the Judge was pleased. It was a disguised "affidavit man," or footpad, no doubt, who had been employed to frighten him. The trick had fallen through.

A "court of appeal," such as the false Hugh Peters had indicated, with assassination for its sanction, would be an uncomfortable institution for a "hanging judge" like the Honourable Justice Harbottle. That sarcastic and ferocious administrator of the criminal code of England, at that time a rather pharisaical, bloody and heinous system of justice, had reasons of his own for choosing to try that very Lewis Pyneweck, on whose behalf this audacious trick was devised. Try him he would. No man living should take that morsel out of his mouth.

Of Lewis Pyneweck, of course, so far as the outer world could see, he knew nothing. He would try him after his fashion, without fear, favour, or affection.

But did he not remember a certain thin man, dressed in mourning, in whose house, in Shrewsbury, the Judge's lodgings used to be, until a scandal of ill-treating his wife came suddenly to light? A grocer with a demure look, a soft step, and a lean face as dark as mahogany, with a nose sharp and long, standing ever so little awry, and a pair of dark steady brown eyes under thinly-traced black brows—a man whose thin lips wore always a faint unpleasant smile.

Had not that scoundrel an account to settle with the Judge? had he not been troublesome lately? and was not his name Lewis Pyneweck, some time grocer in Shrewsbury, and now prisoner in the jail of that town?

The reader may take it, if he pleases, as a sign that Judge Harbottle was a good Christian, that he suffered nothing ever from remorse. That was undoubtedly true. He had, nevertheless, done this grocer, forger, what you will, some five or six years before, a grievous wrong; but it was not that, but a possible scandal, and possible complications, that troubled the learned Judge now.

Did he not, as a lawyer, know, that to bring a man from his shop to the dock, the chances must be at least ninety-nine out of a hundred that he is guilty?

A weak man like his learned brother Withershins was not a judge to keep the high-roads safe, and make crime tremble. Old Judge Harbottle was the man to make the evil-disposed quiver, and to refresh the world with showers of wicked blood, and thus save the innocent, to the refrain of the ancient saw he loved to quote:

Foolish pity

Ruins a city.

In hanging that fellow he could not be wrong. The eye of a man accustomed to look upon the dock could not fail to read "villain" written sharp and clear in his plotting face. Of course he would try him, and no one else should.

A saucy-looking woman, still handsome, in a mob-cap gay with blue ribbons, in a saque of flowered silk, with lace and rings on, much too fine for the Judge's housekeeper, which nevertheless she was, peeped into his study next morning, and, seeing the Judge alone, stepped in.

"Here's another letter from him, come by the post this morning. Can't you do nothing for him?" she said wheedlingly, with her arm over his neck, and her delicate finger and thumb fiddling with the lobe of his purple ear.

"I'll try," said Judge Harbottle, not raising his eyes from the paper he was reading.

"I knew you'd do what I asked you," she said.

The Judge clapt his gouty claw over his heart, and made her an ironical bow.

"What," she asked, "will you do?"

"Hang him," said the Judge with a chuckle.

"You don't mean to; no, you don't, my little man," said she, surveying herself in a mirror on the wall.

"I'm d———d but I think you're falling in love with your husband at last!" said Judge Harbottle.

"I'm blest but I think you're growing jealous of him," replied the lady with a laugh. "But no; he was always a bad one to me; I've done with him long ago."

"And he with you, by George! When he took your fortune, and your spoons, and your ear-rings, he had all he wanted of you. He drove you from his house; and when he discovered you had made yourself comfortable, and found a good situation, he'd have taken your guineas, and your silver, and your ear-rings over again, and then allowed you half-a-dozen years more to make a new harvest for his mill. You don't wish him good; if you say you do, you lie."

She laughed a wicked, saucy laugh, and gave the terrible Rhadamanthus a playful tap on the chops.

 GREEN TEA

"He wants me to send him money to fee a counsellor," she said, while her eyes wandered over the pictures on the wall, and back again to the looking-glass; and certainly she did not look as if his jeopardy troubled her very much.

"Confound his impudence, the scoundrel!" thundered the old Judge, throwing himself back in his chair, as he used to do in furore on the bench, and the lines of his mouth looked brutal, and his eyes ready to leap from their sockets. "If you answer his letter from my house to please yourself, you'll write your next from somebody else's to please me. You understand, my pretty witch, I'll not be pestered. Come, no pouting; whimpering won't do. You don't care a brass farthing for the villain, body or soul. You came here but to make a row. You are one of Mother Carey's chickens; and where you come, the storm is up. Get you gone, baggage! get you gone!" he repeated, with a stamp; for a knock at the hall-door made her instantaneous disappearance indispensable.

I need hardly say that the venerable Hugh Peters did not appear again. The Judge never mentioned him. But oddly enough, considering how he laughed to scorn the weak invention which he had blown into dust at the very first puff, his white-wigged visitor and the conference in the dark front parlour were often in his memory.

His shrewd eye told him that allowing for change of tints and such disguises as the playhouse affords every night, the features of this false old man, who had turned out too hard for his tall footman, were identical with those of Lewis Pyneweck.

Judge Harbottle made his registrar call upon the crown solicitor, and tell him that there was a man in town who bore a wonderful resemblance to a prisoner in Shrewsbury jail named Lewis Pyneweck, and to make inquiry through the post forthwith whether any one was personating Pyneweck in prison and whether he had thus or otherwise made his escape.

The prisoner was safe, however, and no question as to his identity.

CHAPTER - IV

Interruption in Court

In due time Judge Harbottle went circuit; and in due time the judges were in Shrewsbury. News travelled slowly in those days, and newspapers, like the wagons and stage coaches, took matters easily. Mrs. Pyneweck, in the Judge's house, with a diminished household—the greater part of the Judge's servants having gone with him, for he had given up riding circuit, and travelled in his coach in state—kept house rather solitarily at home.

In spite of quarrels, in spite of mutual injuries—some of them, inflicted by herself, enormous—in spite of a married life of spited bickerings—a life in which there seemed no love or liking or forbearance, for years—now that Pyneweck stood in near danger of death, something like remorse came suddenly upon her. She knew that in Shrewsbury were transacting the scenes which were to determine his fate. She knew she did not love him; but she could not have supposed, even a fortnight before, that the hour of suspense could have affected her so powerfully.

She knew the day on which the trial was expected to take place. She could not get it out of her head for a minute; she felt faint as it drew towards evening.

Two or three days passed; and then she knew that the trial must be over by this time. There were floods between London and Shrewsbury, and news was long delayed. She wished the floods would last forever. It was dreadful waiting to hear; dreadful to know that the event was over, and that she could not hear till self-willed rivers subsided; dreadful to know that they must subside and the news come at last.

She had some vague trust in the Judge's good nature, and much in the resources of chance and accident. She had contrived to send the money he wanted. He would not be without legal advice and energetic and skilled support.

At last the news did come—a long arrear all in a gush: a letter from a female friend in Shrewsbury; a return of the sentences, sent up for the Judge; and most important, because most easily got at, being told with great aplomb and brevity, the long-deferred intelligence of the Shrewsbury Assizes in the Morning Advertiser. Like an impatient reader of a novel, who reads the last page first, she read with dizzy eyes the list of the executions.

Two were respited, seven were hanged; and in that capital catalogue was this line:

"Lewis Pyneweck—forgery."

She had to read it a half-a-dozen times over before she was sure she understood it. Here was the paragraph:

Sentence, Death—7.

Executed accordingly, on Friday the 13th instant, to wit:

Thomas Primer, alias Duck—highway robbery.

Flora Guy—stealing to the value of 11s. 6d.

Arthur Pounden—burglary.

Matilda Mummery—riot.

Lewis Pyneweck—forgery, bill of exchange.

And when she reached this, she read it over and over, feeling very cold and sick.

This buxom housekeeper was known in the house as Mrs. Carwell—Carwell being her maiden name, which she had resumed.

No one in the house except its master knew her history. Her introduction had been managed craftily. No one suspected that it had been concerted between her and the old reprobate in scarlet and ermine.

Flora Carwell ran up the stairs now, and snatched her little girl, hardly seven years of age, whom she met on the lobby, hurriedly up in her arms, and carried her into her bedroom, without well knowing what she was doing, and sat down, placing the child before her. She was not able to speak. She held the child before her, and looked in the little girl's wondering face, and burst into tears of horror.

She thought the Judge could have saved him. I daresay he could. For a time she was furious with him, and hugged and kissed her bewildered little girl, who returned her gaze with large round eyes.

That little girl had lost her father, and knew nothing of the matter. She had always been told that her father was dead long ago.

A woman, coarse, uneducated, vain, and violent, does not reason, or even feel, very distinctly; but in these tears of consternation were mingling a self-upbraiding. She felt afraid of that little child.

But Mrs. Carwell was a person who lived not upon sentiment, but upon beef and pudding; she consoled herself with punch; she did not trouble herself long even with resentments; she was a gross and material person, and could not mourn over the irrevocable for more than a limited number of hours, even if she would.

Judge Harbottle was soon in London again. Except the gout, this savage old epicurean never knew a day's sickness. He laughed, and coaxed, and bullied away the young woman's faint upbraidings, and in a little time Lewis Pyneweck troubled her no more; and the Judge secretly chuckled over the perfectly fair removal of a bore, who might have grown little by little into something very like a tyrant.

It was the lot of the Judge whose adventures I am now recounting to try criminal cases at the Old Bailey shortly after his return. He had commenced his charge to the jury in a case of forgery, and was, after his wont, thundering dead against the prisoner, with many a hard aggravation and cynical gibe, when suddenly all died away in silence, and, instead of looking at the jury, the eloquent Judge was gaping at some person in the body of the court.

Among the persons of small importance who stand and listen at the sides was one tall enough to show with a little prominence; a slight mean figure, dressed in seedy black, lean and dark of visage. He had just handed a letter to the crier, before he caught the Judge's eye.

That Judge descried, to his amazement, the features of Lewis Pyneweck. He had the usual faint thin-lipped smile; and with his blue chin raised in air, and as it seemed quite unconscious of the distinguished notice he has attracted, he was stretching his low cravat with his crooked fingers, while he slowly turned his head from side to side—a process which enabled the Judge to see distinctly a stripe of swollen blue round his neck, which indicated, he thought, the grip of the rope.

This man, with a few others, had got a footing on a step, from which he could better see the court. He now stepped down, and the Judge lost sight of him.

 Green Tea

His lordship signed energetically with his hand in the direction in which this man had vanished. He turned to the tipstaff. His first effort to speak ended in a gasp. He cleared his throat, and told the astounded official to arrest that man who had interrupted the court.

"He's but this moment gone down there. Bring him in custody before me, within ten minutes' time, or I'll strip your gown from your shoulders and fine the sheriff!" he thundered, while his eyes flashed round the court in search of the functionary.

Attorneys, counsellors, idle spectators, gazed in the direction in which Mr. Justice Harbottle had shaken his gnarled old hand. They compared notes. Not one had seen any one making a disturbance. They asked one another if the Judge was losing his head.

Nothing came of the search. His lordship concluded his charge a great deal more tamely; and when the jury retired, he stared round the court with a wandering mind, and looked as if he would not have given sixpence to see the prisoner hanged.

CHAPTER - V

Caleb Searcher

The Judge had received the letter; had he known from whom it came, he would no doubt have read it instantaneously. As it was he simply read the direction:

> *To the Honourable*
> *The Lord Justice*
> *Elijah Harbottle,*
> *One of his Majesty's Justices of*
> *the Honourable Court of Common Pleas.*
> *It remained forgotten in his pocket till he reached home.*

When he pulled out that and others from the capacious pocket of his coat, it had its turn, as he sat in his library in his thick silk dressing-gown; and then he found its contents to be a closely-written letter, in a clerk's hand, and an enclosure in "secretary hand," as I believe the angular scrivinary of law-writings in those days was termed, engrossed on a bit of parchment about the size of this page. The letter said:

MR. JUSTICE HARBOTTLE,—MY LORD,

I am ordered by the High Court of Appeal to acquaint your lordship, in order to your better preparing yourself for your trial, that a true bill hath been sent down, and the indictment lieth against your lordship for the murder of one Lewis Pyneweck of Shrewsbury, citizen, wrongfully executed for the forgery of a bill of exchange, on the ——th day of —— last, by reason of the wilful perversion of the evidence, and the undue pressure put upon the jury, together with the illegal admission of evidence by your lordship, well knowing the same to be illegal, by all which the promoter of the prosecution of the said indictment, before the High Court of Appeal, hath lost his life.

And the trial of the said indictment, I am farther ordered to acquaint your lordship, is fixed for the both day of —— next ensuing, by the right honourable the Lord Chief Justice Twofold, of the court aforesaid, to wit, the High Court of Appeal, on which day it will most certainly take place. And I am farther to acquaint your lordship, to prevent any surprise or miscarriage, that your case stands first for the said day, and that the said High Court of Appeal sits day and night, and never rises; and herewith, by order of the said court, I furnish your lordship with a copy (extract) of the record in this case, except of the indictment, whereof, notwithstanding, the substance and effect is supplied to your lordship in this Notice. And farther I am to inform you, that in case the jury then to try your lordship should find you guilty, the right honourable the Lord Chief Justice will, in passing sentence of death upon you, fix the day of execution for the 10th day of ——, being one calendar month from the day of your trial.

It was signed by

CALEB SEARCHER,

Officer of the Crown Solicitor in the

Kingdom of Life and Death.

The Judge glanced through the parchment.

"'Sblood! Do they think a man like me is to be bamboozled by their buffoonery?"

The Judge's coarse features were wrung into one of his sneers; but he was pale. Possibly, after all, there was a conspiracy on foot. It was queer. Did they mean to pistol him in his carriage? or did they only aim at frightening him?

Judge Harbottle had more than enough of animal courage. He was not afraid of highwaymen, and he had fought more than his share of duels, being a foul-mouthed advocate while he held briefs at the bar. No one questioned his fighting qualities. But with respect to this particular case of Pyneweck, he lived in a house of glass. Was there not his pretty, dark-eyed, over-dressed housekeeper, Mrs. Flora Carwell? Very easy for people who knew Shrewsbury to identify Mrs. Pyneweck, if once put upon the scent; and had he not stormed and worked hard in that case? Had he not made it hard sailing for the prisoner? Did he not know very well what the bar thought of it? It would be the worst scandal that ever blasted Judge.

So much there was intimidating in the matter but nothing more. The Judge was a little bit gloomy for a day or two after, and more testy with every one than usual.

He locked up the papers; and about a week after he asked his housekeeper, one day, in the library:

"Had your husband never a brother?"

Mrs. Carwell squalled on this sudden introduction of the funereal topic, and cried exemplary "piggins full," as the Judge used pleasantly to say. But he was in no mood for trifling now, and he said sternly:

"Come, madam! this wearies me. Do it another time; and give me an answer to my question." So she did.

Pyneweck had no brother living. He once had one; but he died in Jamaica.

"How do you know he is dead?" asked the Judge.

"Because he told me so."

"Not the dead man."

"Pyneweck told me so."

"Is that all?" sneered the Judge.

He pondered this matter; and time went on. The Judge was growing a little morose, and less enjoying. The subject struck nearer to his thoughts than he fancied it could have done. But so it is with most undivulged vexations, and there was no one to whom he could tell this one.

It was now the ninth; and Mr Justice Harbottle was glad. He knew nothing would come of it. Still it bothered him; and to-morrow would see it well over.

[What of the paper I have cited? No one saw it during his life; no one, after his death. He spoke of it to Dr. Hedstone; and what purported to be "a copy," in the old Judge's handwriting, was found. The original was nowhere. Was it a copy of an illusion, incident to brain disease? Such is my belief.]

CHAPTER - VI

Arrested

Judge Harbottle went this night to the play at Drury Lane. He was one of the old fellows who care nothing for late hours, and occasional knocking about in pursuit of pleasure. He had appointed with two cronies of Lincoln's Inn to come home in his coach with him to sup after the play.

They were not in his box, but were to meet him near the entrance, and get into his carriage there; and Mr. Justice Harbottle, who hated waiting, was looking a little impatiently from the window.

The Judge yawned.

He told the footman to watch for Counsellor Thavies and Counsellor Beller, who were coming; and, with another yawn, he laid his cocked hat on his knees, closed his eyes, leaned back in his corner, wrapped his mantle closer about him, and began to think of pretty Mrs. Abington.

And being a man who could sleep like a sailor, at a moment's notice, he was thinking of taking a nap. Those fellows had no business to keep a judge waiting.

He heard their voices now. Those rake-hell counsellors were laughing, and bantering, and sparring after their wont. The carriage swayed and jerked, as one got in, and then again as the other followed. The door clapped, and the coach was now jogging and rumbling over the pavement. The Judge was a little bit sulky. He did not care to sit up and open his eyes. Let them suppose he was asleep. He heard them laugh with more malice than good-humour, he thought, as they observed it. He would give them a d———d hard knock or two when they got to his door, and till then he would counterfeit his nap.

The clocks were chiming twelve. Beller and Thavies were silent as tombstones. They were generally loquacious and merry rascals.

The Judge suddenly felt himself roughly seized and thrust from his corner into the middle of the seat, and opening his eyes, instantly he found himself between his two companions.

Before he could blurt out the oath that was at his lips, he saw that they were two strangers—evil-looking fellows, each with a pistol in his hand, and dressed like Bow Street officers.

The Judge clutched at the check-string. The coach pulled up. He stared about him. They were not among houses; but through the windows, under a broad moonlight, he saw a black moor stretching lifelessly from right to left, with rotting trees, pointing fantastic branches in the air, standing here and there in groups, as if they held up their arms and twigs like fingers, in horrible glee at the Judge's coming.

A footman came to the window. He knew his long face and sunken eyes. He knew it was Dingly Chuff, fifteen years ago a footman in his service, whom he had turned off at a moment's notice, in a burst of jealousy, and indicted for a missing spoon. The man had died in prison of the jail-fever.

The Judge drew back in utter amazement. His armed companions signed mutely; and they were again gliding over this unknown moor.

The bloated and gouty old man, in his horror considered the question of resistance. But his athletic days were long over. This moor was a desert. There was no help to be had. He was in the hands of strange servants, even if his recognition turned out to be a delusion, and they were under the command of his captors. There was nothing for it but submission, for the present.

Suddenly the coach was brought nearly to a standstill, so that the prisoner saw an ominous sight from the window.

It was a gigantic gallows beside the road; it stood three-sided, and from each of its three broad beams at top depended in chains some eight or ten bodies, from several of which the cere-clothes had dropped away, leaving the skeletons swinging lightly by their chains. A tall ladder reached to the summit of the structure, and on the peat beneath lay bones.

On top of the dark transverse beam facing the road, from which, as from the other two completing the triangle of death, dangled a row of these unfortunates in chains, a hangman, with a pipe in his mouth, much as we see him in the famous print of the "Idle Apprentice," though here his perch was ever so much higher, was reclining at his ease and listlessly shying bones, from a little heap at his elbow, at the skeletons that hung round, bringing down now a rib or two, now a hand, now half a leg. A long-sighted man could have discerned that he was a dark fellow, lean; and from continually looking down on the earth from the elevation over which, in another sense, he always hung, his nose, his lips, his chin were pendulous and loose, and drawn down into a monstrous grotesque.

This fellow took his pipe from his mouth on seeing the coach, stood up, and cut some solemn capers high on his beam, and shook a new rope in the air, crying with a voice high and distant as the caw of a raven hovering over a gibbet, "A robe for Judge Harbottle!"

The coach was now driving on at its old swift pace.

So high a gallows as that, the Judge had never, even in his most hilarious moments, dreamed of. He thought, he must be raving. And the dead footman! He shook his ears and strained his eyelids; but if he was dreaming, he was unable to awake himself.

There was no good in threatening these scoundrels. A brutum fulmen might bring a real one on his head.

Any submission to get out of their hands; and then heaven and earth he would move to unearth and hunt them down.

Suddenly they drove round a corner of a vast white building, and under a porte-cochère.

CHAPTER - VII

Chief-Justice Twofold

The Judge found himself in a corridor lighted with dingy oil lamps, the walls of bare stone; it looked like a passage in a prison. His guards placed him in the hands of other people. Here and there he saw bony and gigantic soldiers passing to and fro, with muskets over their shoulders. They looked straight before them, grinding their teeth, in bleak fury, with no noise but the clank of their shoes. He saw these by glimpses, round corners, and at the ends of passages, but he did not actually pass them by.

And now, passing under a narrow doorway, he found himself in the dock, confronting a judge in his scarlet robes, in a large court-house. There was nothing to elevate this Temple of Themis above its vulgar kind elsewhere. Dingy enough it looked, in spite of candles lighted in decent abundance. A case had just closed, and the last juror's back was seen escaping through the door in the wall of the jury-box. There were some dozen barristers, some fiddling with pen and ink, others buried in briefs, some beckoning, with the plumes of their pens, to their attorneys, of whom there were no lack; there were clerks to-ing and fro-ing, and the officers of the court, and the registrar, who was handing up a paper to the judge; and the tipstaff, who was presenting a note at the end of his wand to a king's counsel over the heads of the crowd between. If this was the High Court of Appeal, which never rose day or night, it might account for the pale and jaded aspect of everybody in it. An air of indescribable gloom hung upon the pallid features of all the people here; no one ever smiled; all looked more or less secretly suffering.

"The King against Elijah Harbottle!" shouted the officer.

"Is the appellant Lewis Pyneweck in court?" asked Chief-Justice Twofold, in a voice of thunder, that shook the woodwork of the court, and boomed down the corridors.

  GREEN TEA

Up stood Pyneweck from his place at the table.

"Arraign the prisoner!" roared the Chief: and Judge Harbottle felt the panels of the dock round him, and the floor, and the rails quiver in the vibrations of that tremendous voice.

The prisoner, in limine, objected to this pretended court, as being a sham, and non-existent in point of law; and then, that, even if it were a court constituted by law (the Judge was growing dazed), it had not and could not have any jurisdiction to try him for his conduct on the bench.

Whereupon the chief-justice laughed suddenly, and every one in court, turning round upon the prisoner, laughed also, till the laugh grew and roared all round like a deafening acclamation; he saw nothing but glittering eyes and teeth, a universal stare and grin; but though all the voices laughed, not a single face of all those that concentrated their gaze upon him looked like a laughing face. The mirth subsided as suddenly as it began.

The indictment was read. Judge Harbottle actually pleaded! He pleaded "Not Guilty." A jury were sworn. The trial proceeded. Judge Harbottle was bewildered. This could not be real. He must be either mad, or going mad, he thought.

One thing could not fail to strike even him. This Chief-Justice Twofold, who was knocking him about at every turn with sneer and gibe, and roaring him down with his tremendous voice, was a dilated effigy of himself; an image of Mr. Justice Harbottle, at least double his size, and with all his fierce colouring, and his ferocity of eye and visage, enhanced awfully.

Nothing the prisoner could argue, cite, or state, was permitted to retard for a moment the march of the case towards its catastrophe.

The chief-justice seemed to feel his power over the jury, and to exult and riot in the display of it. He glared at them, he nodded to them; he seemed to have established an understanding with them. The lights were faint in that part of the court. The jurors were mere shadows, sitting in rows; the prisoner could see a dozen pair of white eyes shining, coldly, out of the darkness; and whenever the judge in his charge, which was contemptuously brief, nodded and grinned and gibed, the prisoner could see, in the obscurity, by the dip of all these rows of eyes together, that the jury nodded in acquiescence.

And now the charge was over, the huge chief-justice leaned back panting and gloating on the prisoner. Every one in the court turned about, and gazed with steadfast hatred on the man in the dock. From the jury-box where the twelve sworn brethren were whispering together, a sound in the general stillness like a prolonged "hiss-s-s!" was heard; and then, in answer to the challenge of the officer, "How say you, gentlemen of the jury, guilty or not guilty?" came in a melancholy voice the finding, "Guilty."

The place seemed to the eyes of the prisoner to grow gradually darker and darker, till he could discern nothing distinctly but the lumen of the eyes that were turned upon him from every bench and side and corner and gallery of the building. The prisoner doubtless thought that he had quite enough to say, and conclusive, why sentence of death should not be pronounced upon him; but the lord chief-justice puffed it contemptuously away, like so much smoke, and proceeded to pass sentence of death upon the prisoner, having named the tenth of the ensuing month for his execution.

Before he had recovered the stun of this ominous farce, in obedience to the mandate, "Remove the prisoner," he was led from the dock. The lamps seemed all to have gone out, and there were stoves and charcoal-fires here and there, that threw a faint crimson light on the walls of the corridors through which he passed. The stones that composed them looked now enormous, cracked and unhewn.

He came into a vaulted smithy, where two men, naked to the waist, with heads like bulls, round shoulders, and the arms of giants, were welding red-hot chains together with hammers that pelted like thunderbolts.

They looked on the prisoner with fierce red eyes, and rested on their hammers for a minute; and said the elder to his companion, "Take out Elijah Harbottle's gyves;" and with a pincers he plucked the end which lay dazzling in the fire from the furnace.

"One end locks," said he, taking the cool end of the iron in one hand, while with the grip of a vice he seized the leg of the Judge, and locked the ring round his ankle. "The other," he said with a grin, "is welded."

The iron band that was to form the ring for the other leg lay still red hot upon the stone floor, with briliant sparks sporting up and down its surface.

His companion, in his gigantic hands, seized the old Judge's other leg, and pressed his foot immovably to the stone floor; while his senior, in a twinkling, with a masterly application of pincers and hammer, sped the glowing bar around his ankle so tight that the skin and sinews smoked and bubbled again, and old Judge Harbottle uttered a yell that seemed to chill the very stones, and make the iron chains quiver on the wall.

Chains, vaults, smiths, and smithy all vanished in a moment; but the pain continued. Mr. Justice Harbottle was suffering torture all round the ankle on which the infernal smiths had just been operating.

His friends, Thavies and Beller, were startled by the Judge's roar in the midst of their elegant trifling about a marriage à-la-mode case which was going on. The Judge was in panic as well as pain. The street lamps and the light of his own hall door restored him.

"I'm very bad," growled he between his set teeth; "my foot's blazing. Who was he that hurt my foot? 'Tis the gout—'tis the gout!" he said, awaking completely. "How many hours have we been coming from the playhouse? 'Sblood, what has happened on the way? I've slept half the night!"

There had been no hitch or delay, and they had driven home at a good pace.

The Judge, however, was in gout; he was feverish too; and the attack, though very short, was sharp; and when, in about a fortnight, it subsided, his ferocious joviality did not return. He could not get this dream, as he chose to call it, out of his head.

CHAPTER - VIII

Somebody Has Got Into the House

People remarked that the Judge was in the vapours. His doctor said he should go for a fortnight to Buxton.

Whenever the Judge fell into a brown study, he was always conning over the terms of the sentence pronounced upon him in his vision—"in one calendar month from the date of this day;" and then the usual form, "and you shall be hanged by the neck till you are dead," etc. "That will be the 10th—I'm not much in the way of being hanged. I know what stuff dreams are, and I laugh at them; but this is continually in my thoughts, as if it forecast misfortune of some sort. I wish the day my dream gave me were passed and over. I wish I were well purged of my gout. I wish I were as I used to be. 'Tis nothing but vapours, nothing but a maggot." The copy of the parchment and letter which had announced his trial with many a snort and sneer he would read over and over again, and the scenery and people of his dream would rise about him in places the most unlikely, and steal him in a moment from all that surrounded him into a world of shadows.

The Judge had lost his iron energy and banter. He was growing taciturn and morose. The Bar remarked the change, as well they might. His friends thought him ill. The doctor said he was troubled with hypochondria, and that his gout was still lurking in his system, and ordered him to that ancient haunt of crutches and chalk-stones, Buxton.

The Judge's spirits were very low; he was frightened about himself; and he described to his housekeeper, having sent for her to his study to drink a dish of tea, his strange dream in his drive home from Drury Lane Playhouse. He was sinking into the state of nervous dejection in which men lose their faith in orthodox advice, and in despair consult quacks, astrologers, and nursery storytellers. Could such a dream mean that he was to have a fit, and so die on the both? She did not think so. On the contrary, it was certain some good luck must happen on that day.

The Judge kindled; and for the first time for many days, he looked for a minute or two like himself, and he tapped her on the cheek with the hand that was not in flannel.

"Odsbud! odsheart! you dear rogue! I had forgot. There is young Tom— yellow Tom, my nephew, you know, lies sick at Harrogate; why shouldn't he go that day as well as another, and if he does, I get an estate by it? Why, lookee, I asked Doctor Hedstone yesterday if I was like to take a fit any time, and he laughed, and swore I was the last man in town to go off that way."

The Judge sent most of his servants down to Buxton to make his lodgings and all things comfortable for him. He was to follow in a day or two.

It was now the 9th; and the next day well over, he might laugh at his visions and auguries.

On the evening of the 9th, Dr. Hedstone's footman knocked at the Judge's door. The Doctor ran up the dusky stairs to the drawing-room. It was a March evening, near the hour of sunset, with an east wind whistling sharply through the chimney-stacks. A wood fire blazed cheerily on the hearth. And Judge Harbottle, in what was then called a brigadier-wig, with his red roquelaure on, helped the glowing effect of the darkened chamber, which looked red all over like a room on fire.

The Judge had his feet on a stool, and his huge grim purple face confronted the fire, and seemed to pant and swell, as the blaze alternately spread upward and collapsed. He had fallen again among his blue devils, and was thinking of retiring from the Bench, and of fifty other gloomy things.

But the Doctor, who was an energetic son of Aesculapius, would listen to no croaking, told the Judge he was full of gout, and in his present condition no judge even of his own case, but promised him leave to pronounce on all those melancholy questions, a fortnight later.

In the meantime the Judge must be very careful. He was overcharged with gout, and he must not provoke an attack, till the waters of Buxton should do that office for him, in their own salutary way.

The Doctor did not think him perhaps quite so well as he pretended, for he told him he wanted rest, and would be better if he went forthwith to his bed.

Mr. Gerningham, his valet, assisted him, and gave him his drops; and the Judge told him to wait in his bedroom till he should go to sleep.

Three persons that night had specially odd stories to tell.

The housekeeper had got rid of the trouble of amusing her little girl at this anxious time, by giving her leave to run about the sitting-rooms and look at the pictures and china, on the usual condition of touching nothing. It was not until the last gleam of sunset had for some time faded, and the twilight had so deepened that she could no longer discern the colours on the china figures on the chimneypiece or in the cabinets, that the child returned to the housekeeper's room to find her mother.

To her she related, after some prattle about the china, and the pictures, and the Judge's two grand wigs in the dressing-room off the library, an adventure of an extraordinary kind.

In the hall was placed, as was customary in those times, the sedan-chair which the master of the house occasionally used, covered with stamped leather, and studded with gilt nails, and with its red silk blinds down. In this case, the doors of this old-fashioned conveyance were locked, the windows up, and, as I said, the blinds down, but not so closely that the curious child could not peep underneath one of them, and see into the interior.

A parting beam from the setting sun, admitted through the window of a back room, shot obliquely through the open door, and lighting on the chair, shone with a dull transparency through the crimson blind.

To her surprise, the child saw in the shadow a thin man, dressed in black, seated in it; he had sharp dark features; his nose, she fancied, a little awry, and his brown eyes were looking straight before him; his hand was on his thigh, and he stirred no more than the waxen figure she had seen at Southwark fair.

A child is so often lectured for asking questions, and on the propriety of silence, and the superior wisdom of its elders, that it accepts most things at last in good faith; and the little girl acquiesced respectfully in the occupation of the chair by this mahogany-faced person as being all right and proper.

It was not until she asked her mother who this man was, and observed her scared face as she questioned her more minutely upon the appearance of the stranger, that she began to understand that she had seen something unaccountable.

Mrs. Carwell took the key of the chair from its nail over the footman's shelf, and led the child by the hand up to the hall, having a lighted candle in her other hand. She stopped at a distance from the chair, and placed the candlestick in the child's hand.

"Peep in, Margery, again, and try if there's anything there," she whispered; "hold the candle near the blind so as to throw its light through the curtain."

The child peeped, this time with a very solemn face, and intimated at once that he was gone.

"Look again, and be sure," urged her mother.

The little girl was quite certain; and Mrs. Carwell, with her mob-cap of lace and cherry-coloured ribbons, and her dark brown hair, not yet powdered, over a very pale face, unlocked the door, looked in, and beheld emptiness.

"All a mistake, child, you see."

"There! ma'am! see there! He's gone round the corner," said the child.

"Where?" said Mrs. Carwell, stepping backward a step.

"Into that room."

"Tut, child! 'twas the shadow," cried Mrs. Carwell, angrily, because she was frightened. "I moved the candle." But she clutched one of the poles of the chair, which leant against the wall in the corner, and pounded the floor furiously with one end of it, being afraid to pass the open door the child had pointed to.

The cook and two kitchen-maids came running upstairs, not knowing what to make of this unwonted alarm.

They all searched the room; but it was still and empty, and no sign of any one's having been there.

Some people may suppose that the direction given to her thoughts by this odd little incident will account for a very strange illusion which Mrs. Carwell herself experienced about two hours later.

CHAPTER - IX

The Judge Leaves His House

M rs. Flora Carwell was going up the great staircase with a posset for the Judge in a china bowl, on a little silver tray.

Across the top of the well-staircase there runs a massive oak rail; and, raising her eyes accidentally, she saw an extremely odd-looking stranger, slim and long, leaning carelessly over with a pipe between his finger and thumb. Nose, lips, and chin seemed all to droop downward into extraordinary length, as he leant his odd peering face over the banister. In his other hand he held a coil of rope, one end of which escaped from under his elbow and hung over the rail.

Mrs. Carwell, who had no suspicion at the moment, that he was not a real person, and fancied that he was some one employed in cording the Judge's luggage, called to know what he was doing there.

Instead of answering, he turned about, and walked across the lobby, at about the same leisurely pace at which she was ascending, and entered a room, into which she followed him. It was an uncarpeted and unfurnished chamber. An open trunk lay upon the floor empty, and beside it the coil of rope; but except herself there her. Perhaps, when she was able to think it over, it was a relief to was no one in the room.

Mrs. Carwell was very much frightened, and now concluded that the child must have seen the same ghost that had just appeared to believe so; for the face, figure, and dress described by the child were awfully like Pyneweck; and this certainly was not he.

Very much scared and very hysterical, Mrs. Carwell ran down to her room, afraid to look over her shoulder, and got some companions about her, and wept, and talked, and drank more than one cordial, and talked and wept again, and so on, until, in those early days, it was ten o'clock, and time to go to bed.

A scullery maid remained up finishing some of her scouring and "scalding" for some time after the other servants—who, as I said, were few in number—that night had got to their beds. This was a low-browed, broad-faced, intrepid wench with black hair, who did not "vally a ghost not a button," and treated the housekeeper's hysterics with measureless scorn.

The old house was quiet now. It was near twelve o'clock, no sounds were audible except the muffled wailing of the wintry winds, piping high among the roofs and chimneys, or rumbling at intervals, in under gusts, through the narrow channels of the street.

The spacious solitudes of the kitchen level were awfully dark, and this sceptical kitchen-wench was the only person now up and about the house. She hummed tunes to herself, for a time; and then stopped and listened; and then resumed her work again. At last, she was destined to be more terrified than even was the housekeeper.

There was a back kitchen in this house, and from this she heard, as if coming from below its foundations, a sound like heavy strokes, that seemed to shake the earth beneath her feet. Sometimes a dozen in sequence, at regular intervals; sometimes fewer. She walked out softly into the passage, and was surprised to see a dusky glow issuing from this room, as if from a charcoal fire.

The room seemed thick with smoke.

Looking in she very dimly beheld a monstrous figure, over a furnace, beating with a mighty hammer the rings and rivets of a chain.

The strokes, swift and heavy as they looked, sounded hollow and distant. The man stopped, and pointed to something on the floor, that, through the smoky haze, looked, the thought, like a dead body. She remarked no more; but the servants in the room close by, startled from their sleep by a hideous scream, found her in a swoon on the flags, close to the door, where she had just witnessed this ghastly vision.

Startled by the girl's incoherent asseverations that she had seen the Judge's corpse on the floor, two servants having first searched the lower part of the house, went rather frightened up-stairs to inquire whether their master was well. They found him, not in his bed, but in his room. He had a table with candles burning at his bedside, and was getting on his clothes again; and he swore and cursed at them roundly in his old style, telling them that he had business, and that he would discharge on the spot any scoundrel who should dare to disturb him again.

So the invalid was left to his quietude.

In the morning it was rumored here and there in the street that the Judge was dead. A servant was sent from the house three doors away, by Counsellor Traverse, to inquire at Judge Harbottle's hall door.

The servant who opened it was pale and reserved, and would only say that the Judge was ill. He had had a dangerous accident; Doctor Hedstone had been with him at seven o'clock in the morning.

There were averted looks, short answers, pale and frowning faces, and all the usual signs that there was a secret that sat heavily upon their minds and the time for disclosing which had not yet come. That time would arrive when the coroner had arrived, and the mortal scandal that had befallen the house could be no longer hidden. For that morning Mr. Justice Harbottle had been found hanging by the neck from the banister at the top of the great staircase, and quite dead.

There was not the smallest sign of any struggle or resistance. There had not been heard a cry or any other noise in the slightest degree indicative of violence. There was medical evidence to show that, in his atrabilious state, it was quite on the cards that he might have made away with himself. The jury found accordingly that it was a case of suicide. But to those who were acquainted with the strange story which Judge Harbottle had related to at least two persons, the fact that the catastrophe occurred on the morning of March 10th seemed a startling coincidence.

A few days after, the pomp of a great funeral attended him to the grave; and so, in the language of Scripture, "the rich man died, and was buried."

THE END